Sample

MW00882220

behind the
ROCKNG
HORSE

Copyright 2020, Ciana Stone

This book is a work of fiction. Names, characters, organizations, businesses, places, events, and incidents are the product of the author's imagination or are used factiously. Any resemblance to actual persons, living or dead, events, or locales, is entirely coincidental.
Copyright © 2019 Ciana Stone
Cover by Syneca Featherstone
All rights reserved.

Behind the Rocking Horse:

The 7 Bridges Killer

ALL RIGHTS RESERVED

Behind the Rocking Horse© 2020 Ciana Stone

Cover art by Syneca

Edited by Nicole DeVincentis

Electronic book publication June 26,2020

Print book publication June 16, 2020

This book may not be reproduced or used in whole or in part by any means existing without written permission from the publisher, OriginalSyn.

Warning: The unauthorized reproduction or distribution of this copyrighted work is illegal. No part of this book may be scanned, uploaded or distributed via the Internet or any other means, electronic or print, without the publisher's permission. Criminal copyright infringement, including infringement without monetary gain, is investigated by the FBI and is punishable by up to 5 years in federal prison and a fine of $250,000. (http://www.fbi.gov/ipr/). Please purchase only authorized electronic or print editions and do not participate in or encourage the electronic piracy of copyrighted material. Your support of the author's rights is appreciated.

This book is a work of fiction and any resemblance to persons, living or dead, or places, events or locales is purely coincidental. The characters are productions of the authors' imagination and used fictitiously

A Note for Readers:

There are times, in life, when we're all bothered by things happening in the world, things we can't control. The pain and suffering we read about, evil acts people commit against one another, against the innocent – it all weighs on us, tears at the fabric of humanity and makes us fear we're on the road to certain doom.

I think that's sometimes what drives authors to write about hard topics, to face the evil and darkness in their tales and at least try to combat it with words. To state through the actions of our heroes that we do not accept this, that we will fight and will not stop until the evil is vanquished.

We all need heroes – in our tales and in our daily lives. We need to feel that in the end, goodness will prevail, and evil will be crushed. This is a wish for that, a tale of ordinary people who are forced to face extraordinary evil. And hopefully survive.

Dedication:
As always, for the love of my life.

Always and forever. I do.

behind the
ROCKNG
HORSE

PART 1

"Fear is pain arising from the anticipation of evil."

-Aristotle

Prologue

It's over, Isabelle.

I win. If you surrender now, I'll let him live.

Oh God, not again. She thought the last time was bad. Now here she was, once more faced with losing the man she loved, scared to fight, yet without another option. She had to find a way to overcome her fear, or they wouldn't survive.

Are you listening, Isabelle?

How she hated that voice, how she hated him. If only she could stop shaking. Fear was as much her enemy as he. Yet, she couldn't blame it all on him. This was a trap of her own design, one that had, unfortunately, not unfolded as planned.

Every creak of wood, drip of water, or brush of leaves against a window made her heart jump in her chest. A sheen of sweat made her hands slick, and her clothing cling damply to her. Isabelle rose just enough to peer from behind the window curtain.

She didn't see movement outside, but at present, clouds covered the moon, casting the yard in indistinct shapes and varying degrees of darkness that shifted in the wind of the approaching storm.

At her feet lay the man she loved, the man who had already nearly died once trying to save her from this monster. The last time, the monster had used a knife. He'd used one tonight, and now her love's life was on the line once more. Just like eight years ago. Would this nightmare ever end?

The deepest of the stab wounds in his upper back had luckily missed his lung, but she was worried that the second might affect his kidney.

The third, the one in his shoulder, didn't appear to have hit any major arteries but was bleeding profusely and rendered him unable to raise his arm or grip the big 9mm handgun he carried as a service weapon.

She'd done all she could to bind the wounds. With the power shut down and no internet or cell reception, they were cut off. If he was going to survive, she had to figure a way to get them out of there.

The problem was, Isabelle didn't know how. The moment she opened the door, they'd be vulnerable to attack, and she was certain the monster would kill Gib this time. She couldn't let that happen, but she had no weapons. She didn't know how to fire Gib's gun, and even if he told her, she probably couldn't hit the broad side of a barn.

Isabelle, I'm waiting for you.

Come to me, my love.

Don't make me kill him.

Come to me, and he lives. Just take that step, Isabelle. Cross the last bridge that will bring you forever to me.

She sank back down and whispered to Gib, "Maybe if I go outside, you can–"

"No," he cut her off.

She put her fingertips to his lips. "Listen to me. I'm not going to let him kill you, and you know he doesn't want me dead, so this is the best way. I'll make a deal with him. I'll make him call for an ambulance, and then I'll go with him."

"So he can put you back inside a cage? Iz, don't. We'll fight him together. Just help me get my gun from the holster."

4

"Gi–"

"No, you listen. Take my gun from the holster and do exactly as I say. You can do this."

For a split second, she hesitated. The part of her that was terrified to lose him said to just leave him there. Leave him and go make a deal with the devil so Gib could live.

The part that was trying not to scream in terror at the idea of being a prisoner to the monster told her to take the chance. If she killed the beast, it was over. They were free, and the long nightmare could end.

"Do it, Iz. For us. Let's end this."

"Yes," she agreed, letting herself succumb to her own darkness and need for the terror to end. "Yes. Tell me what to do."

Within moments they were ready. She was ready. For the first time in her life, she willingly opened herself, allowing the evil to hear her.

I have to see you. Face-to-face. Come inside.

She waited, trembling, and felt her hands grow wet with sweat. The gun felt too heavy, too big. If he came in, could she pull the trigger? Could she hit him?

Isabelle watched the door until she was nearly blind, and everything seemed to merge into a featureless blur of shadow. When the door handle moved, making a slight click, she almost wet her pants.

The door opened, and a darker form within the gray moved across the threshold. Two more steps and the cloud cover shrouding the moon lifted. Light from the window to her left slanted across two tall figures. Between them was a tiny figure, a child whose hands were in the grips of not one but two monsters.

All the air went out of Isabelle's lungs, and she nearly dropped the gun.

"Oh, dear God." It was worse than she could have imagined.

"Shoot him, Iz," Gib panted the words, every moment, every breath an effort.

Come, her monster urged. *I promise I'll let him live. I'll let them both live.*

"Iz, shoot him!"

"I said come!" the monster's twin roared, this time for real, not just in her head.

Isabelle screamed, raised the weapon, and pulled the trigger. It flashed brightly in the darkness, making spots of light dance in her vision, and the report of the gun made it impossible to hear.

She felt someone grab her, trying to take the gun, and she pulled the trigger again. Almost simultaneously, there was another shot. And then the world exploded into an endless sea of white.

Chapter One

January 3rd, 2020

The past held her prisoner, refusing to release
her. She didn't want to remember, to sink back into
the night her life changed, but sometimes memories
refused to be ignored. Like now.

Unable to banish the thoughts, she let them claim
her.

"Shhh, now. If you talk like that, I'll have to hurt
you. Do you understand?"

Of course, she didn't.

She didn't understand any of what was happening.
One minute she was playing Super Mario Brothers

with Donny in his room, and now she was in the middle of a nightmare.

Donny's tears tore at her heart. He loved that game. It didn't matter that sometimes it stopped working, or that the old television it was hooked to had lost its color, and often half of the screen vanished.

That old television would never display Mario after today. The bad man, all dressed in black with the scary black mask, kicked the screen out. He laughed when he did it because it made Donny cry. He must enjoy making people cry. Mama was crying and begging him to leave, or to please let her children go.

That obviously made him mad because he shouted at her to shut her mouth or he'd cut her tongue out. Mama went white as a sheet. Donny peed his pants, and she almost threw up.

Almost. But her Dad had taught her to stand up to bullies and not let them rattle you, so she yelled at him to leave her mama alone.

That made the bad man angrier, and he started beating on her mother, punching her in the face and the belly. She wanted so much to help her mother, but there was nothing she could do since she was tied up, just like Donny.

All she could do was yell at the bad man, call him

names and say how her Dad was going to kill him when he found out. That she would kill him if he untied her.

That took his attention off her mother, and onto herself.

She would soon find out the cost of her actions, and the price was one she'd face every day for the rest of her life.

Isabelle screamed her way to consciousness and struggled to wake, climbing through the fog of sleep as the terrors fought to keep her trapped in the memory.

Isabelle.

She sat straight up in bed with her heart hammering in her chest and a cold sweat forming on her body.

Her eyes moved, searching the darkness as her hands clenched into tight fists. There was nothing amiss. Her room looked no different now than when she fell asleep.

But appearance often lies, and this was one of those times. Everything was different now. She knew she hadn't dreamed that whisper. She'd feared it her entire life, knowing that each time he gave her respite, the moment would come again when she'd feel him reaching out for her. Call.

There was never a time she could just relax, stop standing guard on her walls, watching for the monster. She couldn't let her guard down because she couldn't predict when he'd reach out again, brushing her mind with his whisper.

Now the time was upon her, and she could barely function from the terror. Her breath was ragged, and sweat dampened her nightshirt and made her hair stick to her skin.

Isabelle.

She knew she couldn't acknowledge the call. It was imperative she keep her barriers in place, to hide behind those mental walls she'd constructed. It was the only way to stay safe, the only way to keep him from locating her again.

Happy New Year, my love.

I've waited a long time, Isabelle. Soon it will be our time. You'll cross the final bridge, and then you will be mine.

No. She would not.

Bile rose in her throat, and she bounded off the bed and to the bathroom. By the time she was bent over the toilet, the need to vomit had dissipated, but her heart still pounded, and her skin felt clammy. She recognized what was happening.

A panic attack.

It'd been a while since she'd had one, and she knew what to do to combat it, so she went back to the bedroom, sat cross-legged on the floor in a patch of moonlight, and forced herself to focus on one thing. Breathing.

In and out. Inhale for a slow three-count, exhale for a slow six-count, and with every three cycles, increase the length of the exhale.

By the time her exhale count reached seventeen, the attack had abated, but the whispers were still there, just at the edge of her perception. Intelligible, but audible, like the buzz of an insect from afar.

Confident she was now in control, she remained where she was. Thinking. Why now? Was it because this was the anniversary of the night he killed her family? Or had he been calling out to her all along and had just now broken through to her mind?

What had changed to weaken her mental barriers enough for him to breach her defenses?

The answer came to her immediately. She was alone.

Lonely.

That annoyed her. She should be stronger, able to stand on her own.

After all, it wasn't just herself she was protecting.

That thought acted like alchemy, transforming her fear into anger, and strengthening her resolve, allowing her to fortify her defenses. She felt the barrier grow denser, solidifying until it was as strong as iron forged in the fires of hell.

Her body was drenched and trembling before the whispering faded into nothing. Even then, she delayed, scared it might be a ruse.

After several long hours, she felt safe enough to stop pouring her strength into the barrier.

That's when the memories closed in on her. Like a hungry pack of wolves, they circled, snapping and growling, growing ever closer until finally, they overwhelmed her. Images and sounds pounded her, wearing her down.

She saw it all again, felt every awful moment. No, not every moment. Why was it that no matter how many times the memories imprisoned her, there were gaps?

Just out of reach. She'd tried many techniques,

undergone hypnosis, regression therapy, and a host of others, but nothing would summon those missing moments.

Unexpectedly, it became clear. Finally, after all these years, she understood. It was *him*. He didn't want her to remember. If she did, then she *would* have something to tell the police or FBI, and he couldn't allow that.

With effort, she pushed the memories back down into the dark, seeing them disappear in a swirl, down the drain, and into the deep well before she closed the lid and locked it.

Then she rose, stripped off her wet nightshirt, and picked up the smooth worry stone from her nightstand. She walked over to open the window, letting the night air whisper over her skin. As much as she'd hoped to escape this path, she realized now she had no choice.

Isabelle.

She grimaced.

She'd known he'd try again, thinking her too weak to endure another assault tonight. Isabelle was smart enough to realize that something had to have taken place to prompt him to reach out.

He'd left her alone for a year.

She sensed that he'd done so to try to lull her into a false sense of peace. To make her believe he was finished with her. That way, when his whisper came in the night, it would provoke a higher level of terror because she thought it was over.

Isabelle? I know you can hear me.

Do you still hear them? Your mother and your brother? Do you hear their screams of anguish? Do you still dream about it? About me? Can you still feel me? Feel the touch of my hands, the searing pain of the blade as it sliced through your eyes?

Or perhaps those old memories have faded, been replaced with thoughts of our last special time together. I thought perhaps you'd be ready for me, but you'd sullied yourself with that man. I had to redeem you, you understand. You're my special girl, my true love.

I'm happy that you've finally come to your senses and banished the men you allowed into your life who do nothing but let you down or disappoint you. Perhaps this past year of reflection has finally shown you they're not your destiny.

We've crossed many bridges together, my love. From that first one, when I claimed you until you turned your back on me in favor of him.

I have forgiven you. I will accept your apology and your submission when the time is right.

Isabelle felt the hate rise, and she latched onto its heat, letting it replenish her resistance. He wanted to believe she could care for him, but she never would. She'd used her respite from his contact to work on ways to strengthen her ability to thwart his attempts to penetrate her mind and locate her.

A flash of light in her mind brought a revelation, one she'd prayed for and thought she'd be denied.

Miraculously, she felt the acrid heat of her hatred fade. This epiphany made her weak with gratitude, then amazingly filled her with power.

Izzi felt a bit ashamed to not have realized it before now. She no longer needed her hatred for strength. She wasn't a frightened child anymore, or even a terrorized young woman, unsure of her own ability to fight. Now she knew where to find her power. Where it'd been all along, waiting for her to recognize and accept.

He was a creature of the dark and gained his power from it. She was his opposite. A child of the light. The one place where he held no sway.

Isabelle's eyes lost all color, and she dove into the light that flowered like the opening of a blossom for her. Here she found assurance that he'd not laid claim to her soul.

Nor would he ever.

She'd never forget or forgive, and one day, she would destroy her monster, watch him blaze like dry tinder until not even his ash remained. *That* was her destiny. She just wasn't sure when she'd find the courage and strength to physically face him again. Today definitely wasn't the day. As much as she longed for it, the time had not yet come when she was secure in her ability to best him.

And until she could eliminate all fear, she couldn't win. So how did she dismiss the fear and dread? The problem was the anticipation of what *might* happen seemed to constantly gnaw at her. She tried to remember the last time she felt safe, powerful enough to battle the monster.

It came to her, and the memory brought tears. She almost sunk into self-pity, almost wailed to the fates, *Why me?* She'd never understood why her life had been filled with so much horror and pain. Was it some kind of karmic debt she had to pay? If so, she prayed every day she'd paid in full.

She wanted a life, one that had no monsters whispering in her mind, one where the man she loved was by her side. One where she was just a normal woman, living an ordinary life with a husband and maybe children.

What a sweet dream.

She didn't know if destiny would grant her that. All she could do was wish and try to find ways to bolster her courage so that when the time came, she could banish the monster once and for all.

And with luck, survive to seek that life she so desperately wanted.

Chapter Two

February 14, 2020

It was going to be a perfect evening. He could feel anticipation singing in his veins, putting a spring in his step. Were it not for the fact he had no desire to attract attention, he'd have been tempted to do like the old song from the classic film his father had loved and "whistle a happy tune."

Not that he needed the act of whistling to feel happiness rise like effervescent bubbles inside him. Everything was perfect, just as planned. The quarry had been chosen wisely, as always, to get the most pleasure possible from the evening.

It was a Valentine's gift. While he wouldn't be spending it with the woman he wanted, he would, nonetheless, think of her every moment, and imagine her bearing witness to the events of the evening.

And one day, he'd share these special moments with her. He was currently rethinking his methods of winning her devotion but knew their time would come. Until then, these missions satisfied his cravings and helped him to stay at the top of his game. And on the top of the FBI's most-wanted list.

He took pride in that accomplishment.

Tonight, he'd completed his first mission of the new year. He thought about it as his footsteps crunched on the gravel of the narrow path. It'd taken a bit longer than expected to locate the perfect candidate, and he deliberately chose one he felt would put his skills to the test.

The location had to fit a strict set of parameters. He was utterly inflexible on those requirements and would not budge even a fraction from the rules he'd established. Even if the woman was a perfect candidate, if the location of her home did not meet his criteria, he moved on.

Finding the right woman was more complicated than anyone would imagine. First, she had to be a mother with small children living in the home. Her partner, or ex as the case might be, had to be someone who offered little support and wasn't interested in exercising custodial privileges.

Meeting this strict criterion and locating the perfect

target was a challenge and he prided himself on meeting challenges. He enjoyed pushing himself and each time he made a selection, he felt a sense of pride.

Seducing the woman was the easy part and definitely in his wheelhouse. He prided himself on being able to read a woman and know how she'd respond and how fast she was willing to let things progress between them.

He preferred women who were ready to invite him into their homes and beds within a couple of weeks.

More than that, and he quickly grew bored.

This month's delectable was harder to win than he'd expected, but by the time twilight fell on Valentine's Day, the woman's handsome new suitor was walking up to her front steps. A leather duffle bag was slung over one shoulder, and he carried a dozen roses in a crystal vase in one hand.

Naturally, there was red tissue paper covering the glass. Leaving a fingerprint would be unacceptable. He thought back to his mentor, and all the times he'd had to clean up after the man.

Those mistakes would not be attributed to him. History would record that fact. The most prolific serial killer in the history of man, and the smartest.

The one who was never caught.

That thought made him smile. He was still smiling when she opened the door.

"For you." He offered the flowers.

The smile of happiness and lust she rewarded him with was amusing. Soon that would change, and she would give him what he craved.

Her pain and fear.

February 15, 2020

It was a day of potential. A day to choose happiness in whatever form it was offered. But then what day was not? She reminded herself of that daily. Like morning prayers, it was her mantra. Sooner or later, it would take hold and become part of her instead of something she had to remind herself to strive for.

Isabelle looked around as she walked across the side yard to a large planting bed near the driveway. She'd meant to get it weeded for some time and if she didn't pay attention to it soon, once spring arrived, the weeds would choke out her flowers. Funny how weeds always seemed to be much hardier than whatever she planted.

She smiled as it dawned on her that the concept held true for mental gardens as well. You had to stop the negative before it became too rooted. Once it was well dug in, it grew robust and could choke out your mental well-being and happiness, leaving you scared, angry, or just unhappy.

Her smile faded as she considered all the times she'd held on to her negative. A lot of work had gone into ridding herself of that habit. She couldn't claim she'd achieved success, but with luck, one day she'd be free of it. Until then, she'd continue to be mindful and put in the effort.

The sound of a plane passing overhead had her shielding her eyes and looking up. It was unseasonably warm today, hovering in the mid-sixties. Fluffy clouds decorated the field of blue above. As she watched, the plane disappeared into one of those clouds. She closed her eyes for a brief moment, remembering what it felt like to fly through clouds.

Her first time experiencing it had been like something from a dream. Being enveloped in clouds, out of touch, literally, with the earth. She liked it and was scared of it at the same time. That, and other flights, taught her she was a creature of the earth. She liked being grounded, feeling the earth beneath her feet, being able to dig her fingers and toes into the soil.

Like she would do today. She opened her eyes and

smiled. Yes, this was a good day to be outside. Tomorrow could be back down into the thirties, so she'd make good use of the beautiful weather while it lasted.

Isabelle towed her garden cart to the edge of the flower bed, removed a five-gallon orange bucket from the cart to put weeds into, pulled on her gloves, and knelt. There was something calming and peaceful about working in her flower and herb gardens. She'd spent many hours this last year working outside, searching for and soaking up whatever peace and serenity was available to her.

For a time, she turned her attention to her weeding, setting her mind free. Thoughts came and went, and she observed and noticed but didn't settle on any single one. Instead, she recognized things she'd circle back to later for more in-depth reflection.

She thought perhaps she'd reached a milestone in her healing. At least she thought that until she felt the change in the air. *The wind of change.* The corners of her mouth rose as she considered how many people over the years had smiled at her for such statements. Until they realized her words were not made in jest, nor were they a boast.

Isabelle's senses were… different. Maybe it wasn't even that. Perhaps she'd just been forced as a child to develop insights that everyone had, but rarely used.

Most people adhere to the assumption that humans have five basic senses: touch, sight, hearing, smell, and taste. The sensory organs associated with each of these senses send information to the brain to help us perceive and understand the world around us.

Because of the unique nature of her childhood, she developed additional senses. It was those "extras" that inspired Isabelle to dig deeper into potential human abilities. She needed to convince herself that she wasn't a freak, and that quest had netted knowledge she'd used as stepping-stones to discovery.

Her first breakthrough came from reading a paper that stated some scientists believe all humans have far more than five senses. The exact number was and is still a point of disagreement. Most of those familiar with the subject agree there are between fourteen and twenty, depending upon how one defines a sense.

Isabelle used the most straightforward definition. That a sense is a channel through which your body can observe itself or the outside world.

That definition was one she felt became metaphorically etched in stone at the age of sixteen, her first year in college, thanks to a parapsychology lecture she sneaked in to observe, being given by one of the top researchers in the field.

Since that day, her definition had held firm, and her knowledge base had grown. That comprehension was what helped her to let go of perceptions others ascribed to her and to accept herself, without the label, "freak."

Now, what some would call her psychic ability alerted her to the fact that a visitor would soon arrive, and would, quite likely, put her boast of achieving peace to the test.

Less than five minutes later, a car rounded the curve in the long drive and slowed to a stop near her garden cart, currently blocking the driveway. Isabelle looked up, and the driver's side door, which was on the opposite side of the driveway from where she sat, opened.

Some things never change. The first time she set eyes on Gibson Foster, it took her breath.

Time hadn't dulled the effect he had on her. She peeled off her gloves and stood.

"Iz."

At thirty-two years old, Isabelle had heard her name, or some diminutive form of it spoken thousands of times, possibly tens of thousands. It'd been voiced in compassion, friendship, anger, jest, praise, flirtation, condemnation, threat, and lust, but no one had ever spoken her name like Gib.

When he spoke her name, it sounded like a prayer, a deep-seated wish-given sound. It thrilled and humbled her, made her weak and not just physically.

Her resolve threatened to evaporate like mist in sunlight. Dear God, where was her strength when she needed it the most?

"Gib." She found her tongue.

He closed the car door and walked around to the front of the vehicle. She'd forgotten what a striking figure he cut. Standing three inches over six feet, Gib carried his two hundred plus pounds well. Slim in the waist with a full chest and muscular arms, he gave the impression of strength and power, a commanding presence.

And was still as handsome as the day she met him, despite the added gray in his hair and the short, Van Dyke beard that adorned his face.

"Iz, I…" He reached up to rub his index finger and thumb over his beard, from the corners of his mouth, downward. She recognized the motion. It signified he was at a loss for words, which didn't happen often.

He didn't need words.

27

She knew why he was there. For her, but not for them.

"The answer is no." She gave an answer before he could ask.

"Can we at least talk about it?"

"To what end?"

"So that I can say my piece and know I did everything I could to stop this bastard. At least give me that."

"Fine." She tossed her garden gloves onto the cart, turned, and headed for the house.

Gib followed, thinking of the reason he'd come here today. There'd been a murder in Mississippi, one that matched the pattern of an Unsub the FBI have been trying to capture for decades. The Seven Bridges Killer.

In 1995, a series of grisly murders earned the Unsub the title of the Seven Bridges Killer. Over eight months, seven families were destroyed. In each instance, a mother and her children were murdered, and something—an organ or body part–was taken from the mother and left, along with the murder weapon, hanging on a nearby bridge.

Because the items were found on seven different bridges, law enforcement assumed the location of the bridges held significance. So far, that theory had neither been substantiated nor refuted. The Unsub had, however, become something of a legend. To date, there'd been no other evidence found at a murder scene. No material or trace that would lend clues to his identity had ever been found. Not one.

The knifes used to murder the victims were ones taken from the homes of the victims; thus, all trace evidence led back to the family.

Three times, Gib convinced Isabelle to help them catch this killer. The first time, she fell in love with him.

Gib wasn't ignorant or blind. He knew it was happening. Hell, he might even have encouraged it, if he was completely honest. They started as friends, or at least that's how he wanted to remember it. Maybe the truth was, he was attracted to her at first glance.

Nevertheless, he was married, and despite having feelings for her, he didn't want to screw up his life or break up his family. Isabelle didn't hold that against him. But then things went south, people died, and after admitting she was in love with him, she returned home and took a job teaching. He went on with his life, trying to fool himself into believing he was over her.

The next time another member of Gib's Unit, Leo Grant, almost died. Isabelle and Leo had history. He was the first member of the BAU to meet her, the first to be her friend and for a time, her lover. She told Gib once that when she thought Leo would die, it made her realize that her monster would never stop. With him, it was kill or be killed. That's when she decided she wanted the monster to die.

It just didn't happen. A few years later, the Unsub kidnapped her. It took Gib and his team three months to find her. Gib nearly died saving her. Izzi confessed to him that she saw it for what it was, that she was a danger to all of them. They were safer without her around. So, once he healed, she left again and returned home again to North Carolina.

She hadn't spoken to him since.

Gib wasn't psychic, but it didn't take special abilities to know that she didn't want any part of an investigation dealing with what she called her monster. Gib wasn't stupid or insensitive. Isabelle was the only known survivor of the Seven Bridges Killer. He'd deliberately let her live after blinding her. Luckily her sight was restored through surgery and since that time, her senses had multiplied, taken on more power.

Isabelle was convinced there was some kind of psychic link between her and the Unsub. She feared if she helped the FBI with the case again, the killer would know and would make sure to hurt or kill someone she cared for. She thought that's why Gib and Leo almost died. Gib didn't discount her feelings or her conviction about the psychic connection. He'd seen too much to write it off. But he still needed help and had to try.

Her back was ramrod straight as she walked in front of him. He noticed she was thinner than the last time he saw her a year ago. She'd also cut her hair. A year ago, it'd reached her waist. Today it was just past her shoulder blades, falling in uneven layers, giving her that look she had when they first met.

A nymph from the forest, or a fairy princess.

As if hearing his thoughts, she looked over her shoulder at him, and when she did, she stumbled. With one slightly larger than normal step, he had hold of her, sweeping his arm around her for balance. Then without thinking, he pulled her close.

For a moment, they were frozen, gazes locked, and bodies pressed together. Feelings he'd spent a year trying to quell raced to the surface, expunging all the effort that had gone into putting a lid on them.

"Don't."

It wasn't an admonishment but a plea, and one he understood because of the feelings rampaging inside him.

"Please."

Gib released her, and they continued to the house. Once there, she led him to the back porch, mounted the steps, kicked off her shoes, and opened the kitchen door. He followed her in and stopped just inside the door.

All houses have smells, the leftover odors from cooking, the residuals of cleaning solutions, washing detergents, dryer sheets, perfumes, furniture polish, and a host of other scents. Izzi's house always smelled like a blend of sweet herbs and spices, both energizing and calming, despite the dichotomy of that description.

Perhaps he perceived it that way because until a year ago, it'd been his home away from home, the place they came to escape the world.

"Coffee?" she asked. "Tea, iced water?"

"No, thanks."

She fixed herself a glass of iced water and turned to him. "Porch?"

Gib stepped aside and gestured for her to precede

him. She did and took a seat on the porch swing. He followed and hesitated until she patted the seat beside her.

He sat and was struck, not for the first time, by how small she was. Her feet dangled free, not touching the floor. From habit established some time ago, he started slowly rocking them.

"Do you remember the first time you came here?" she asked, took a drink from her glass and then set it on the table beside the swing.

That question took him back twelve years.

Chapter Three

As long as his mind functioned, Gib would remember. At that time, he was thirty-six years old and just starting his new position as special agent in charge of unit four of the Behavioral Analysis Unit of the FBI. Being young and new to the position, he was eager to make a name for himself, and took things seriously. Deadly serious, as his wife, Diana, often scolded, and added as a warning.

"Just don't take it so seriously you put yourself six feet under from the stress. It's not worth your life, honey."

Gib thought about Diana's warning, and about the day that Isabelle Adams became part of his life.

2008 - Quantico, Virginia

Gib crammed his hands in his trouser pockets and rocked back and forth on his heels. He was mad enough to hit something. Or someone. But he wouldn't. He'd work through his anger and deal with the situation like a professional.

He'd almost curbed the worst of the irritation when a knock sounded at his door. Gib knew who it was. "Come," he called without turning around.

Leo Grant, his most experienced agent and friend, entered and waited just inside the door.

"Close it, please."

Gib heard the door close, but waited a beat before turning to face Leo. "Have a seat, Special Agent Grant."

Leo's expression and slight nod let Gib know Leo was fully aware that this conversation was strictly professional. Having Gib as his superior was new for both men. Until a month ago, they'd been on equal footing, Special Agents assigned to the Behavioral Analysis Unit, under the leadership of Special Agent in Charge, Mike Smithers.

Mike retired, and Gib was selected to fill his shoes. Gib was thrilled, excited, and more than a little eager to show his worth. He'd thought things were going well until this week. Now he realized he hadn't been very observant. How had it escaped him that one of his best friends and teammate was having an affair?

Once Leo was seated, Gib walked over and settled into the chair behind his desk, letting the expanse of wood separate them figuratively as well as literally.

"I asked you here to discuss your request to enlist the aid of Dr. Isabelle Adams in this investigation, Agent Grant."

"Yes, sir."

Gib tried to ignore the awkwardness he felt at hearing Leo address him as sir. "Something has been brought to my attention that we must address. I will ask this once. Did you have any kind of sexual relations with her when you interviewed her in 2005?"

"No, sir."

"Are you now engaged in a sexual relationship with her?"

There was a moment's hesitation before Leo's gaze locked with his, and he answered. "Yes, sir."

"Was she of age when this affair began?"

"Yes, sir."

"When did it begin?"

"Six months ago. We met again when I did the lecture at UNCC. She's twenty, sir. Almost twenty-one. And a professor at the university."

That relieved Gib. At least partially. If Gib became

aware that Leo was involved with an underage girl, he'd have no choice but to bring Leo up on disciplinary charges. Since the young woman was an adult in the eyes of the law, there would be no need for that. But it bothered Gib, nonetheless.

He'd known Leo and Leo's wife, Margaux, for a long time. Because of their friendship, Gib was aware of the problems Leo and Margaux had been going through for the last couple of years. To his credit, Leo kept his personal life out of the workplace and, to the best of Gib's knowledge, had never allowed his marital problems to interfere with his job.

"Stepping out of my role as SAC and speaking as a friend, I have to ask. Why?" Gib needed an answer. The last thing he wanted was to lose respect for his friend.

Leo shook his head and slumped in his chair. "I wish I could find the words. She's… she's not like any woman I've ever known. Good heavens, Gib, look at all she's suffered. How many among us could have carried such a burden without becoming damaged beyond repair?"

Gib knew the facts, had suffered more than one bout of revulsion and sense of wonder at all Isabelle Adams had endured. But he knew her only from words on a page and old photos. "Tell me about her."

"She's amazing. Intelligent, educated, and informed... and—psychic."

"So, you said. Would you care to elaborate?"

"Izzi has a way of knowing things without being told. She's allowed me to see medical and scholarly reports written about her, and a host of scientists and medical researchers agree that she possesses what we might call extra senses. She's also connected with the killer. She's afraid to do it, but convinced she can touch his mind if she lowers the mental barriers she's spent her life erecting and fortifying."

"And you believe this?"

"I do."

Had that statement come from anyone else, Gib might have dismissed it. Coming from Leo, it carried weight. The fact that the Seven Bridges Killer had now killed two more women and three children put Gib in a circumstance of some urgency. This psychopath needed to be stopped, and he'd use every resource available.

That thought brought a slight pang of shame. If the reports Leo mentioned held up under scrutiny, then Isabelle Adams might well help them solve a case that started in 1995. It would certainly be a feather in Gib's cap if they succeeded in that task. If he didn't close cases, he could lose the position of command. If his team outperformed expectations, he and everyone under his control could expect pay grade increases and the potential to rise higher in the BAU.

Gib made a decision.

"Back to business. Put me in touch with Dr. Adams. I want to pay her a visit and speak with her in person. If things pan out, we'll bring her in as a consultant."

"Yes, sir."

Gib nodded. "Dismissed." He hoped he wasn't making a mistake. "Leo, hold on," he hurried to add as Leo stood. "As a friend, I'd like to ask you to stay a moment."

"Sure," Leo agreed and sat again.

"Why?" Gib asked.

"Didn't we already cover that?"

"Not really. Why cheat on Margaux? I know you've been through a few rough years, but your marriage has to be worth saving."

Leo nodded, looked down for a moment, and then up at Gib. "It is. I want to but... Gib, I'll never forget the day I first saw her. You remember. It was 2005 and we thought the Seven Bridges Killer was starting up again. It'd been a decade, and suddenly in four months, there were two more families killed, and everything matched the '95 killings."

"I remember. You volunteered to go interview the girl who survived the string of murders in '95. Isabelle Adams."

"I never expected to be so–affected. I remember reading about her and what happened to her and her family, but I wasn't quite prepared for the young woman I met."

"She was how old then?" Gib asked. "Sixteen? Seventeen?"

"Seventeen. A sophomore in college. She was sitting on a bench, waiting for me. There were pairs or groups of students in the commons, all talking, having lunch, making out with their boy or girlfriends. She sat alone, reading.

"But she looked up before I reached her and watched until I stopped in front of her. "Agent Grant," she said. "I didn't think you'd be so tall. Or so sexy. Is that common for BAU agents, or are you an anomaly?'"

"I didn't quite know what to say, so I just extended

my hand to her.

"Thank you for agreeing to speak with me, Miss Adams," I said.

"She stood, removed her sunglasses, took my hand, and looked up at me and God as my witness, I actually stepped back in shock."

"Shock?"

"Her eyes. I've never seen anything like that. Not white, not green, but... a kind of pearlescent that has hues of pale sea green and blue.

"Her hair was very dark before her family was attacked, and her eyebrows and eyelashes remained dark, which makes the contrast with her eyes even more pronounced.

"Her hair was cut short, like some kind of pixie from a fairy tale and I swear to you, she looked just like something from a book, a fairy princess or–what was that little fairy? Tinker Bell? She seemed... otherworldly."

"But you didn't see her again after that?" Gib needed reassurance.

"No. I thought about her over the years but never attempted to contact her. Although she told me we'd see one another again. I didn't really believe it, but I guess she was right because the day I did that lecture just before the end of the year at UNCC in 2008, there she was. All grown up and the most beautiful thing I've ever seen in my life."

Leo held up his hand as Gib opened his mouth to speak. "I love my wife, Gib. I've always loved her, but I could no more have said no to Isabelle than I could have shot myself. She told me we had six months, and then our time would end. I didn't believe her, but I should have."

"Why is that?"

"Because tomorrow is the anniversary of the day of that lecture. And tomorrow, I'm guessing, is the day you'll go see her and decide whether to use her as a consultant."

"And that will put an end to the affair?"

"Yes, I believe it will."

"How do you feel about that? And I'm asking as a friend."

"Sad. Grateful. I know I need to repair the damage to my marriage, and I swear to you I will try. Because you're my friend, I'm going to ask a favor, and it's a big ask.

"Don't let Margaux know about this. About Izzi. She

might survive finding out I'd had an affair, but if she ever met Izzi, she'd leave me."

"Isabelle Adams can't be that special."

"Tell me that after you meet her, my friend."

Gib nodded, stood, and rose to walk around the desk and offer his hand to Leo. "You have my word."

"Thank you."

Leo took his hand, grasped tight for a moment, then released it. "I owe you."

"Friendship doesn't require payment, Leo. You know that."

"Still, I owe you. Anything else, sir?"

Gib sensed Leo's need to fall into a professional role and honored the unspoken request. "No, thank you. If you'll contact Dr. Adams and ask permission for me to call, I'll speak with her and make arrangements to fly to North Carolina tomorrow and meet with her."

"I'll do that now."

"Thank you."

Now, Gib pulled back from the memory. Leo had been right. Meeting Izzi was a pivotal moment in his life. He never imagined that day they met, that in time she'd become a ruling passion in his life. He was happily married, intended on staying that way, and despite the powerful effect she had on him, he and she had never crossed the line from friends to something more.

She didn't have a lot of friends, it had seemed. No one really to confide in. She may have taken the breakup with Leo as something that was inevitable, but when she talked about it, he paid attention to the space between her words and heard someone who was lonely and a bit heartbroken.

His wife, Diana, always said his soft heart got him into trouble all the time. Perhaps she was right because he felt sorry for Isabelle Adams. She was so young and had suffered so much. At almost twenty-one, she was alone. All her family was gone, and she was not ordinary enough to have an easy time fitting in.

That sympathy prompted him to become her friend, someone she could confide in. Strangely, it ended up that she was as much, if not more, of a confidant and sounding board for him than the other way around. She had a way of seeing into people that brought things into the light they weren't always aware they were hiding.

Still, they were friends only. That's how it was meant to be.

Or so he thought.

Gib pushed back the thoughts and asked what he'd been holding back for a long time. "Do you wish I'd never shown up that first day?"

She reached over to take his hand. "I don't blame you for what happened. You must know that."

"But it cost you your relationship with Leo and—"

"Shhh," she silenced him. "Leo and I were never meant to be together forever. He loves Margaux. He always did. They'd just lost sight of what they wanted the most. When I said yes to the request to work with your team, he and I both knew that was the end of whatever we had. It took a bit of time to figure out new dynamics, but lucky for me, our friendship survived, and I was lucky enough to eventually become friends with his wife and daughter, Alanna.

"It took a little while, but before long, Margaux became cautiously trusting. They still walked on uneven ground for a long time, but when he was hurt, it made her realize how important he was to her. That's what he really wanted, all along. To be important to her.

"It worked out the way it was supposed to for them. Besides, I found a friend to help me through my rough patch—and you really did, you know—so it worked out for me, too."

"I think I received far more than I gave," he spoke from the heart. "I never planned on loving you, Iz, even though I did, and you knew it. Still, I'd never thought we'd end up together. And maybe that was a mistake. Maybe I should have never told you. Maybe then that monster wouldn't have taken you. I swear I never–"

"Don't." This time, Izzi's hand tightened on his. "I told you then, and it still holds true. No one forced me to get involved. It was my decision. I should have known better."

Gib nodded and was silent for a time, trying to decide if he should be there at all. What right did he have to ask for her help?

Again. After all she'd been through.

"He'll know if I get involved in the case with you, again," she whispered. "I don't know how, but somehow he knows."

"Leo and Galen are working the case. I'm supervising. You'd be working with them and the rest of the Unit."

"But not you?"

"You said you'd never work with me again."

"Only because I love you. If I do this, people I care about may die. I don't know if I can live with that. Especially you. I know Diana was your first love, your wife, and the mother of your children, and I'll never be to you what she was, but you were and are my first. And only."

"What about Leo?"

"Leo was a crush. I knew it then. I love him, but was never in love with him."

Gib was silent for a bit, trying to figure out what was the right thing to do. He knew Izzi's skills and had no doubt she could draw out the killer, get his attention, and maybe with all the team working together, they could trip him up, force him to make a mistake.

If so, they could stop him. Once and for all.

"Would it change anything if I promise I'll protect you? I swear, I will. Even if it means 24-7 protection. I won't let him hurt you, Iz."

The next squeeze she gave his hand was gentle. "Don't you get it? It's you who needs protection. He's playing with you. With all of us."

"You think killing innocent women and children is playing?" Gib immediately regretted the anger that was so obvious in his voice.

"I think it is for him. And he won't quit."

"He will if we stop him. Help us do that. Help me."

"Why do you think we can? We failed before. People died. You almost died. Do you think this time is any different?"

"I do. Our team is strong, determined, and smart. You know that. Leo and Galen are the best Agents in the BAU. Fiona is a top-notch profiler, and Tamara and David are both brilliant. The point is, if we work together, we can not only find him, we can stop him. For good.

"Please. I know I have no right to play on your emotions, to ask you to do this because of how you feel about me, about our past, but I need you, Iz. I have to stop this monster, and I can't do it without you."

Izzi pulled something from her pocket, something very familiar. Her worry-stone. Once upon a time, he'd thought it was something she used to calm herself, or perhaps focus her attention. Then he realized it was that, but also more. If she handed it to him after she'd used it, it would be almost too hot to touch, and literally vibrating with energy.

She sat there, staring out over her yard, rubbing her thumb lightly over the worn surface of the stone. Gib wondered if she was ignoring him. Then she turned her head, and for the first time since they sat, she looked at him. Had it been the first time he'd experienced it, he would have been taken aback, but he'd been locked in her gaze before, seen her eyes go white.

"We won't catch him. The time for the final showdown isn't now. This is just another act in the play, one more demonstration that he's smarter than all of you. You're playing his game, and he's not about to let you win."

She blinked, and her eyes were once again normal. At least normal for her. "But I can help you with the Cheerleader Killer."

"How do you know about that?"

"I don't, but you do. Can you use my help?"

"Yes, with both, if you're willing."

She nodded. "I'll help you all I can."

"Will you come to Virginia so you can work with the team daily?"

"And live where? In a hotel? You know I don't fare well in hotels."

"You can stay with me."

"Gib, I–"

"I have a guest room. You're welcome to it. Please, Iz."

He wondered if she noticed the way he addressed her since he arrived. Iz. No one called her Iz but him, and he hadn't used that diminutive since the day she walked away from him. She smiled at him, and he sensed a hint of relief in her expression at his offer and an acceptance of him using his own unique version of her name.

"Thank you. I'll consider the housing offer and let you know. But not today. Today, we're going to walk the woods, eat a good home-cooked meal, and you're going to hold me while I sleep, and we'll pretend, just for tonight, there are no monsters to battle."

"Is that what we're about to do?"

"Yes."

Gib smiled, stood, and offered her hand. "It is permissible to hold hands while we take that walk?"

"Absolutely." She placed her hand in his and let him tug her to her feet.

"I've missed you, Iz." He couldn't stop himself from speaking, even knowing that he shouldn't. "I love you, you know."

"And I'll never love anyone the way I love you. Love was never the issue."

Gib remembered the last time she said that. It was right before she told him she couldn't go on, chasing monsters, being saturated in evil and death. She had to get away from it and asked that he leave with her.

He couldn't let go.

Of his position, or the work.

And so, he lost her.

Right now, he wondered if that was the stupidest decision he'd ever made.

Chapter Four

Cabarrus County, North Carolina

Izzi didn't want to sleep. The feel of Gib's big body spooned up around her, his arm over her, holding her snugly, was better than any dream. She'd missed him more than she wanted to admit, even to herself.

Gib was her first and only love. Not the only man she'd been intimate with, but the only one she'd given her total trust and heart. To say he'd betrayed that love and trust would be a lie. He'd never promised to put her wants or desires ahead of his own, so when he refused to leave the BAU, she hadn't been surprised. Just disappointed.

And heartbroken.

Tonight, she lay in the bed they'd once shared and thought about their path to this point in time.

Gib would never have come to ask for her help if he

had another option. She wondered if Leo had anything to do with it. It was Leo who'd convinced Gib to come here twelve years ago and enlist her assistance.

Look where that had led them. All of them. They'd not captured the killer, and Leo almost died. And just when they'd recovered, and it seemed life was going to cut them a break, she got caged in hell by the killer and nearly lost Gib when he came to save her.

Those weeks, sitting in that hospital, not knowing if Gib was going to live, was worse than being the prisoner of a monster.

Could she do it again?

Face that fear?

Her first reaction was probably the wisest. Say no and don't back down. But the truth was, now that she'd seen Gib, now that she could feel his arms around her, she didn't know if she could let him leave without her.

She'd thought she could find happiness without him. She was wrong. Not a day passed she hadn't thought of him, missed him, and, more times than not, regretted her decision.

Why then, was she so reluctant to say yes to his

request?

Answers weren't likely to present themselves
tonight, maybe not at all. Perhaps it wasn't a matter
of doing what she wanted, but what was right.

That's always the position Gib chose.

What was right? What served the greater good?

Izzi closed her eyes and tried to stop the chatter of
her own mental voice. Morning would come soon
enough, and then she'd decide.

For now, she'd allow herself to sleep in the arms of
the man she loved and pretend there were no
monsters to hunt.

Just as she started to drift off, her sense of peace
shattered.

Isabelle.

Her eyes flew open, and her body tensed. She felt
Gib shift behind her and willed her body to relax.

I know you can hear me.

I can almost sense your thoughts.

In time I will.

You know I'll come for you.

You're mine, after all.

That did it. Fury blossomed with the heat of a bomb. She wouldn't be goaded into lowering her shield. She knew that's what he wanted. If she did, he'd connect his mind to hers, and she'd be laid bare. But that's not how it was going to be.

For the first, in a long time, genuine resolve returned, along with a deep-seated need. She'd be damned if he would reach her. Not until she was ready. Not until she'd set a trap he couldn't avoid or escape.

And then, she'd destroy him. Utterly and completely.

Izzi rolled over to face Gib, waking him in the process. "Are you okay?" She could hear the concern in his voice.

"I am. For the first time in a long while I am. I'm going with you, Gib. And this time we're going to end him."

"You mean, catch him."

"No, I mean end him. It's the price of my help."

He looked into her eyes for a long moment, then nodded. "Then, so be it. If you're sure."

"I've never been more sure about anything..." She nearly chickened out but then finished what was in her heart and mind. "Except that I love you."

"Does that mean you'll live with me?"

"I'll live in your house. In the guest room you offered. That's as far as I'm willing to commit on a personal level while we're working together."

"Why? Because you don't trust me?"

"No," she interrupted gently. "Because I need to know that *he* can't tap into anyone else's mind, and I don't want him to know I'm involved – with the BAU or with you."

To her relief, she didn't get an argument. Quite the opposite. "That's smart, and I agree. I'm just grateful you said yes. To going back to work with me. I don't want you to think I expected–"

"I know," she interrupted. "And I'm not saying we won't end up together. I hope in time we will."

"In time?"

She smiled at him. "Yes. When all this is done. It's what I want more than anything.

"Then let's destroy a monster, Dr. Adams."

"That's the plan, Special Agent in Charge, Gibson Foster. Starting first thing tomorrow. For now, hold me while I sleep."

"With pleasure."

Isabelle rolled over and felt the warmth of his body as he held her. She thought about what was to come, and that turned her memories of how she'd initially become involved with Gib and his team.

Quantico, Virginia

While Gib was with Isabelle, his team was working. They'd put in another sixteen-hour day and everyone was exhausted. Leo Grant and Galen Morris walked out together. It was well past midnight. They, like the other members of the team, had gone over all the evidence on the latest murders, reading every report and interview, and they knew nothing more about the Seven Bridges Killer than when they started.

To say they were all frustrated was an understatement. They were ready to pull their hair out and were downright pissed that a team of highly trained professionals could be outsmarted by a serial killer.

"What are we missing?" Leo asked as they exited the building.

Galen stopped, took a deep breath, and let it out slowly. "From everything we know about forensics, the chance of someone committing this type of crime and not leaving behind any evidence, trace, or material is as close to impossible as it gets."

"And yet, that's exactly what we run up against time after time with this killer," Leo pointed out.

"At the risk of sounding redundant, it isn't possible," Galen insisted. "We know that – it's a scientific improbability of such high degree that it rises to an impossibility. Particularly when you consider the nature of the crimes. These aren't simple crimes. This killer is organized, methodical, and skilled."

He raised his hand as Leo opened his mouth. "I know what you're going to say. No one is that skilled. I agree. Look at all we know about investigative techniques and forensics. Do you think either of us could pull off such a crime without leaving behind one bit of evidence?"

"No."

"Well, there you go." Galen threw up his hands. "Let's use that as a given, and where does it take us?"

"I'm guessing you're going to tell me."

"You bet your ass I am. It takes us back to my

original assertion. We've missed something. Or something has changed. He left evidence this time."

"So, he screwed up?" Leo asked.

"I don't believe for a second he screwed up. Why, after all this time, would he leave evidence?"

"I don't guess he would – unless he's getting sloppy. Or…"

He didn't want to finish the thought, but duty dictated he do just that. "Or we missed something before."

Leo was pretty sure he knew what was coming next, but felt Galen needed to get it out. He'd been every bit as frustrated as the rest of the team. "What's our next step?" Leo asked.

Galen cut his eyes in Leo's direction. "We go back to the beginning."

"We already did that." Leo didn't want to go back to the beginning. He didn't want to go anywhere but home, to crawl into bed and sleep for twelve hours. But he knew his partner. Galen wouldn't let go of this, so the best course of action was to take the time, talk it out, and see if they could come up with something – anything– that had not been considered before. "We spent the last sixteen hours going over it from start to finish."

"No, not the beginning of the latest crime. The beginning. 1995."

Now that was a trip Leo didn't want to take. "We already did that. In 2005 and again in 2008, and –"

"Yes, I know," Galen interrupted. "But our process was flawed."

"Flawed? How so?"

Galen gestured toward his car. "Come on, let's go get a drink."

Leo knew better than to argue. "Fine." He fell in step with his partner. "Tell me how our process was flawed."

Galen looked over at him. "You're not going to like it."

"Tell me anyway."

"Fine. Two words. Isabelle Adams."

"Izzi?" Leo stopped walking. "Izzi was the flaw?"

The look Galen gave him took him aback. "Man, you have a blind-spot the size of Texas when it comes to her. Of course, she was the flaw."

Galen then started walking, and Leo picked up his pace to catch up. "Explain it to me how she could have been a flaw?"

"Because you fell for her, and that colored your judgment."

Leo didn't like that statement. Not at all. Nor did he believe it to be true. He'd always prided himself on being level-headed, favoring reason over emotions. "You know that's not true. She did help us. Look what happened."

"Exactly my point. Look what happened. Marty died. You and Gib both nearly died. Different times but there was a common element at play in every scenario. Isabelle Adams was involved."

"Are you forgetting she was lucky to have survived the 2018 fiasco?"

"Not at all. And that's part of the point. I'm not sure you or Gib is capable of being clear-headed when she's around. It's like she has some kind of spell on you."

"That's bullshit, and you know it."

"Is it?" Galen pressed the unlock button on his key fob and got in the car.

Leo settled into the passenger seat, fastened his seat

belt, and considered the question. Before he could answer, Galen added, "Just think about it. I'm going to. At least until we get to Smithy's. Then tell me I'm wrong."

"Fine."

Leo turned his head to stare out of the window and, for the first time in years, let his thoughts move back in time.

2005, Quantico Virginia
Behavioral Analysis Unit

The team was assembled in the conference room, waiting on Gibson Foster, the Special Agent in Charge of their Unit. At the table sat Agents David Bainbridge and Angela Waterman.

Leo and Galen Morris, his best friend and partner, stood in front of the window. Leo's hands were crammed in the pocket of his slacks, while Galen fiddled with a metal puzzle, twisting and turning it in his hands without even looking at it as he and Leo talked too quietly to be overheard.

They all worked for the National Center for the Analysis of Violent Crime, or NCAVC, which is part of the Federal Bureau of Investigation. As part of the Behavioral Analysis Unit, their focus was on crimes against adults, often, serial killers.

Gibson, or Gib as he asked to be called, had not yet arrived, even though it was he who'd called them in for this special assignment.

The conference room door opened. Gib walked in, followed by Martin Baxter, or Marty as he chose to be called, the team's data analyst and research specialist, a young man who'd been with the unit a little over six months.

Gib gestured toward a table off to one side of the room, and Marty immediately started setting up his laptop. "Good morning," Gib addressed everyone. "Please, sit. As soon as Marty is ready, we'll get started."

No one wasted time taking a seat. Leo cut a look at Gib. Was his expression serious or something more?

Grim. That's the first word that came to mind.

But why? This must be one hell of a case to bring that kind of expression to Gib's face.

A moment later, Marty's soft voice broke the silence in the room. "Ready, sir."

"Thanks, Marty." Gib gave Marty a nod that somehow conveyed gratitude and respect. That was something Leo had learned early about Gib. He always thanked his team for their efforts and, in doing so, continuously earned their devotion. Not that Leo believed it was meant in that manner. Gib was simply a man who recognized the efforts of others, and not bothered in the least when someone else shone brighter at a task or revelation.

Gib watched as Marty started handing out folders to everyone at the table. Once that was done, Marty returned to his seat beside the computer. Gib waited a beat, then looked around at everyone. "Leo? I believe you and Galen have studied this particular serial killer, correct?"

Leo looked up from the inside page of the folder. "Yes, that is correct. Speaking for myself, of course. Galen?" He already knew the answer, but figured the best move was to let Galen answer for himself.

Galen nodded. "Yes. I read the case files on this string of killings."

"Thank you," Gib looked at the others. "For those of you who have not read the case files, everything is in your folder, and you'll need to make yourself familiar with it. Immediately. Before I release you to start that process, Marty has prepared a briefing, and now, I'll turn things over to him."

The big screen on the wall at the end of the table lit, and an image appeared of a small white house with black shutters, cordoned off with crime scene tape.

"To the best of our knowledge, a series of murders that would come to be known as the Seven Bridges killings began in Alabama in 1995." As he talked, photographs of other houses along pictures of signs with the name of the towns displayed. "We believe the killing spree began in Lock Five, Alabama, as you can see marked on the map. There a woman and her eight-year-old son were killed in their home. The woman was married, but her husband was away, helping to move his grandfather into a retirement home."

Leo knew the course of events by heart. He and Galen had discussed this serial killer many times, not hoping he would resurface and hurt more innocent people, but that something would spark new interest, and they could work the case. Galen was convinced between the two of them, they could find the Unsub and carve a notch in their belts at having solved a case that had been on the books for years.

Now, by an unfortunate twist of fate, they were being handed their wish. Leo almost felt guilty for ever having hoped to be assigned to the case.

"As you'll read in your information packets, the Seven Bridges Killer as this Unsub has been dubbed, is particularly barbaric, and doesn't leave anything aside from those he wants law enforcement to find," Marty said.

"He–at least we believe it to be a man–was given this moniker for one of the following reasons.

"First, all the murders take place within a 25-mile radius of a bridge. Second, the Unsub leaves the murder weapon hanging from a bridge along with a body part cut from the adult female victim, and third, there were seven mass murder sites in the 1995 killing spree."

Marty paused, took a sip of water from a plastic bottle he'd placed on the floor beside his chair, then began again. "We can't be sure the murders of 1995 are the first this Unsub committed. There are other unsolved murder cases, but none that are a match to these, which follow almost a ritualistic pattern.

"As I stated previously, there were originally seven mass murders attributed to the Seven Bridges Killer. In each one, the killer gained access to a home where a married woman with children was alone. In each instance, the woman was either divorced, or her husband was away from home for one reason or another. There were no signs of forced entry, indicating that the victims invited the killer into the homes.

"In every event, the children were found bound, and their eyes glued open. It is believed that the children were made to watch as their mother was sexually abused, raped, sodomized, and then murdered. They were then killed as well.

"The killer takes something from each woman and seems to favor removing the heart and does so while the victim is alive, but in one instance, he removed the eyes as well. As incomprehensible as it is, he leaves the blade used to remove the heart on a bridge nearby, hanging with the heart, so that it will attract attention.

"Every murder weapon tested nets the same results. The blood of the victims, partial prints belonging to the female victim or her spouse, and remnants of food items."

Angela, the forensic psychiatrist, looked away from the displayed image on the big screen to address Marty.

"Pardon if I'm jumping too far ahead, but the information on the final case indicates that one of the children was left alive?"

"Correct. A girl. Isabelle Adams. Seven years old. He didn't kill her, but he did cut both of her eyes. The corneal scarring was so extensive, she was declared legally blind, but she eventually was given corneal transplants, and her vision was restored."

"And it says here that her eyes changed colors?" David, a forensic pathologist, looked up from reading to ask. "I've never heard of anything like that."

"Not just her eyes," Marty replied. "Which did change from hazel to an almost translucent pale green, but her hair fell out within a week of the event, and when it grew back in, it was no longer dark brown, but white."

"I see there's additional information," David said. "Leading me to assume that follow-up has been done recently on this girl?"

That's when Gib took charge again. "Yes. There have been two events in the last six weeks, both of which have similarities to the Seven Bridges killings. I asked Marty to do some research, and he found out that the girl who survived, Isabelle Adams, is now seventeen and a sophomore in college."

"A little young to be a sophomore," Galen offered.

"She graduated high school early. As our documentation shows, Isabelle was sent to live with her grandparents after her mother's murder. Her father closed their home but didn't sell it. He was killed two years after her mother and brother were murdered – a drunk driver pulled out in front of his rig, and he went off an embankment, trying to avoid hitting the car.

"Isabelle inherited the house, but as yet it has not been sold. She continued to live with her grandparents, and her grandmother died when she was fifteen, the same year she graduated high school. Her grandfather died before she finished her freshman year."

"Talk about a tragic life." Angela looked at the image frozen on the screen of the little girl, her dark hair pulled back in a ponytail and bandages covering her eyes.

"Is there a recent photo?"

The image on the screen changed. Almost as one, everyone in the room froze. Leo could have sworn he heard a collective inhale. No surprise. Isabelle Adams had definitely changed. Petite in build, her hair was worn in a pixie kind of cut, framing her face. In the photo, she was walking, looking back over her shoulder almost as if sensing she was being watched.

She was beautiful. No, that was the wrong word. She looked like something out of a fantasy or a fairy tale.

Yes, that was it. She had the look of some mystical being, a fairy princess, as silly as it sounded, young, innocent, and exotic

Except for those eyes. There was nothing innocent or young in those pale eyes. Her eyes were those of someone who had seen too much evil. Leo snapped back from those thoughts. It wasn't like him to think in these terms.

What was it about this girl that provoked such thoughts?

Suddenly, he was curious.

Someone was going to have to interview this girl.

That someone was going to be him. It had to be.

Why?

He didn't have a clue, and it didn't matter.

"So, what now?" he directed the question to Gib.

"Now we get started. I need feet on the ground ASAP. We'll interview all law enforcement, medical examiners, friends of the families, teachers, and daycare workers who knew the children, anyone, and everyone connected with any of the murder victims. Marty has prepared a schedule and divided the locations between us. He and I will be going to the site of the most recent killings to make sure everything is being recorded and fed into our database."

Leo took that moment to speak up. "I'd like to interview Miss Adams."

"Hunch or curiosity?" Gib asked.

"Does it matter?"

"Always. I'd bet on your hunches, but we have no time for curiosity. So, which is it?"

Leo glanced again at the image of Isabelle Adams on the screen, then met Gib's gaze without blinking. "Hunch."

Gib nodded and looked at Marty. "Make it happen."

At a nod and quick "yes, sir" from Marty, Gib stood. "Okay, people, the clock is ticking. Let's get to work."

Gib turned, left the room, and Galen leaned over a bit toward Leo. "Why interview the girl?"

"Everyone has a story. I want to hear hers."

"Isn't her interview in the packet?"

"I want to hear it from her lips."

"You want to look her in the eyes and see if she's honest."

"Am I that predictable?"

"Not to most, but I've known you a while, and I know you have that lie detector thing going for you. After all the times you've called bullshit on me, I should know what you're up to."

"I only call bullshit on you when you come up with lame excuses for the bad decisions you make with women."

Galen laughed and stood. "Sure, buddy. It has nothing to do with being jealous of all the action I get."

"You're right; it doesn't. And you're right about my BS meter. I need to look in her eyes and hear her tell it."

Even as he said the words, he knew them to be a lie. He didn't doubt that Isabelle Adams would tell him the truth. That wasn't what he wanted to know. He wanted to know what she saw and felt and smelled before the killer took her sight. He wanted something he could use to find this psycho and either stop him or put him in the ground.

He didn't care which.

Leo returned to the present, looked out of the passenger window, and considered what Galen said.

Was Izzi a detriment to their investigation, or was she the best chance they had at stopping this psycho?

He knew for a fact the killer would respond to Izzi, would reach out to her if she lowered her mental barriers. The Unsub had proven, time and again, that if there was one thing he wanted, it was Isabelle Adams. He had a thing for her Leo didn't understand and probably would feel sick to his soul if he did understand.

Izzi was the one person who could probably goad their killer into action. It was his opinion that they put that to use.

Then again, he couldn't help remembering what it felt like to be stabbed and left to bleed out on the floor. Or how it was Izzi who had found him, plastered her hands over his wounds and screamed for help, keeping him alive until help arrived.

Nor would he forget the teammate they lost, or how Gib nearly died. Maybe there was some validity to Galen's claim. But even if Izzy was a flaw, she was still the best connection they had to this Unsub.

Which meant Leo supported Gib's decision to try and enlist Izzi's help. He, like Gib, had a personal vendetta to settle with this monster, and despite wanting to see justice served, he was honest enough to admit that in this case, he wanted blood.

Ending this monster would allow him to finally sleep well again.

Chapter Five

Cabarrus County, North Carolina

After trying every technique she knew to help her fall asleep and failing each time, Isabelle gave up. When she did, the most remarkable thing happened. For the first time in years, she sensed Leo. It was almost as if his mind was reaching out to her. She opened herself mentally and felt him.

He was remembering. She allowed herself to follow him, to let the memories take her. Izzi smiled as she drifted back in time. It was her sophomore year at the University of North Carolina in the spring of 2005, and she was seventeen years old.

2005

The University of North Carolina at Charlotte

"Stud alert."

Izzi heard the comment from the group of girls sitting together on the grass behind her. They giggled and then, as if sharing a collective mind, started chattering all at the same time.

She looked up from her reading. One glance and she knew who all the girls were giggling and whispering about. She couldn't say she blamed them. He was, in her opinion, magnificent. She supposed handsome, sexy, or some other such adjective would have been applicable but didn't seem quite strong enough of a description.

She watched from behind the dark lenses of her sunglasses, admiring the strong lines of his face, the smooth way he moved as if the act of walking required little effort or perhaps that gravity had less hold on him than everyone else. She wasn't sure what it was, but there was something unique about him. Powerful and attractive.

When his gaze locked on her, she jerked a bit. Agent

Grant. It had to be. She was expecting an Agent Grant from the Behavioral Analysis Unit to meet her here.

She'd been quite enchanted with his voice, that smooth deep tone, and the unmistakable but slightly watered-down British accent.

His appearance was every bit as attractive as his voice. Izzi was especially glad she'd chosen this place. She wasn't at all sure she'd be comfortable being somewhere more private. Here there was noise and movement and distraction, and she suspected she'd need a bit of all of that. This was a place where students often sat on benches along the sidewalk to study, visit with friends, spend time with people they were dating, or flirting with those they'd like to date.

Being younger than everyone else, she was rarely there for anything other than studying or reading. Sometimes she just needed to be outside and feel the sun on her skin. Today that skin was feeling a little warmer than usual, and she suspected it had something to do with the dark-skinned man walking toward her.

"Isabelle Adams?" He stopped in front of her.

"Yes."

"Agent Leo Grant." He showed her his identification.

She took it and scrutinized it before returning it to him. "May I sit?" he asked.

"Of course," she agreed and made room on the bench.

He sat, angled toward her. "I appreciate you taking the time to speak with me, Miss Adams."

Her gaze connected with his, and she bolted to her feet. She might be just shy of eighteen, but she knew what it felt like to be attracted to a man, and right now she'd liked to jump Agent Leo Grant. "Would you mind if we walk?"

"That's fine." He stood and waited for her to slide her book into her book bag and shrug the straps over her shoulders. "Lead the way."

Izzi pointed to the left. They walked for a few yards in silence before she dared to look at him again. "You want to ask me about that day, don't you?"

"Yes, I do."

"Why?"

She could tell her question surprised him because of the minute falter in his pace and the expression on his face. "Pardon?"

"Evade much?"

Izzi immediately scolded herself mentally for teasing an adult, and especially a federal agent, and directed her gaze to her feet. "Sorry, but I was questioned so many times I started to feel like a recording stuck on an endless loop. Then it stopped, and I was finally left alone. At least until another murder happened."

She looked directly at him. "Why do you want to question me now, Agent Grant?"

"I'm hoping there's something you've remembered over the years that you may not have told anyone."

That wasn't the truth.

She could see it in his eyes and really hated that Agent Grant lied to her. Then she realized why he'd lied, and that awareness made her legs feel suddenly weaker than a moment ago.

"He's back, isn't he?" Even she could hear the thickness in her tone, feel the way her throat tightened. The thought that he was back prompted a memory of the whispers that had been part of life, off and on, since she was seven. It made her queasy and sweaty. She wiped one hand over the leg of her jeans.

Agent Grant looked away for a moment, stuck his hands into his trouser pockets, and appeared to be focused on the pavement beneath his feet. Izzi didn't say another word. He'd either answer or not. How he responded wouldn't change anything. She'd known this day would come, tried to wish or pray it away, all the while knowing she'd be unsuccessful. He'd told her they weren't finished. What if he'd decided that now was the time to pick up where they'd left off?

When Agent Grant stopped suddenly, she kept going for two steps before stopping to turn and face him.

"We think he may be starting up again," he said. "But can't be certain, so we're going over everything and talking to everyone involved in the...".

Izzi felt sorry for him when he trailed off and stood there looking at her with an expression of discomfort on his handsome face. "The murders," she filled in the blank for him.

"Yes. Sorry. It must be difficult to hear me speak of it."

She wasn't quite ready to reveal how she felt about any of it. First, she wanted to know how honest Agent Grant would be with her from this point on. "Can I buy you a coffee? There's a nice coffee shop just off-campus. It's only a mile or so if you don't mind the walk."

"I'd be happy to have coffee with you, but perhaps

we could ride. I have a rental car. Providing, of course, you feel safe being in a car with me. If you like, you can call Quantico and verify my identity."

Izzi shook her head. "I don't need to do that. And I'm fine riding with you. Where are you parked?"

"Behind the library."

"This way," she pointed.

They walked in uncomfortable silence. Izzi wasn't quite sure what to make of Agent Grant, aside from being shockingly handsome, soft-spoken, and seemingly, kind and polite. But people often went out of their way to behave in a manner that engendered trust. Once you trust someone, you let your guard down.

And that's what opens the door to them finding the weapon they need to hurt you.

She knew that all too well. A memory surfaced, driving the point home.

> She'd been with her grandparents for over
> six months. Even at seven, she knew she
> was a burden. Her eyes hadn't yet
> sufficiently healed to have surgery, so she
> was technically blind. She could see light
> and shapes, but only as fuzzy blobs. It was

challenging to navigate around the house and had taken a month before she could feed herself without making a huge mess.

One of her grandmother's friends, a lady from the church, stopped by every week or so and often brought her granddaughter, Chelsea, who was a year older than Izzi.

Izzi was thrilled to have someone close to her own age to spend time with. She started to think of Chelsea as her friend.

Until one Sunday, after church, she was holding her grandfather's hand while grandmother chatted with a friend, and Izzi heard Chelsea's voice. "You won't believe why she wears those glasses."

The burst of chatter from multiple voices let Izzi know that Chelsea was with girls from the Sunday school class. A moment later, Chelsea continued. "A bad man killed her mom and brother and cut her eyes up. She can't see hardly at all, and my mom says she'll be a freak for the rest of her life. Just a burden on her poor old grandparents."

Izzi pulled back from the memory, and she realized Agent Grant was watching her. "Have I upset you, Miss Adams?"

"No."

"Your expression would suggest otherwise."

"No, you haven't upset me. I was just thinking."

"About? Oh, here we are, the gray four-door sedan." He pointed to a car.

Once they were in the car, he turned to look at her. "You were thinking?"

Izzi pulled her worry stone from her pocket. Some girls always had a mirror, lip gloss, a hairbrush, or some type of make-up with them. For Izzi, it was her worry stone. Her grandfather gave it to her when she first went to live with him and her grandmother and her nights were filled with terrors and her days with anxiety.

He explained that all she had to do was hold the stone between her index finger and thumb and gently move her thumb back and forth over it. Pop told her it would suck the anxiety right out of her body, and she wouldn't have to be afraid.

As a child, she believed what he said, and

miraculously it worked. As long as she held that small gemstone, rubbing lightly, she could keep the monsters at bay. Now, she looked out of the car window, gathering her courage to talk to Agent Grant, and wishing the stone had the power to make her feel less nervous.

He was very handsome. Sexy. And she wasn't accustomed to being in the company of attractive older men. The guys her age who showed her attention were the ones who tended to be on the fringe, into drugs, and the kind of music that gave her a headache.

She wasn't opposed to smoking pot, but the one time she'd tried acid, she screamed for a day. Izzi wouldn't make that mistake again. She kept her wits about her. And she wasn't the kind of girl who wanted to indulge in meaningless sex. Maybe she'd just chosen badly, but so far, the sex she'd experienced was nothing to brag about or repeat.

"So, you said you were thinking?" Leo prompted again, steering her thoughts back to the memory. She didn't see any harm in telling him, so she related it.

He was quiet for a few moments, then said softly. "People can be unintentionally cruel at times."

That comment, spoken softly, emboldened Izzi to lower the mental walls she kept carefully in place, battened and locked tight. The moment she did, she saw Agent Leo Grant, saw him for who he was – the person, not just the agent, and that insight changed everything. She knew beyond all doubt that she could and would trust him with her life.

And he with hers. In time.

"Yes, they can," she agreed. "And intentionally at others."

"Have you suffered from a lot of that, Miss Adams?"

"You can call me Izzi."

"Izzi? Is that the name you prefer to go by?"

"No. Everyone calls me Isabelle. Izzi was my brother's name for me. My grandparents called me Isabelle. It sounds quite grown up and possibly a bit refined.

I don't feel much like either. I'd rather have my hands in the soil, ride without a saddle, and wear faded denim than dress in the latest fashion with designer labels and spend my energy trying to be pretty."

"But you are, Izzi. Pretty, I mean."

"No, I'm not." She removed her glasses and couldn't help but note the way his eyes widened slightly before he composed himself. "I'm unusual, I guess is the best word."

"Otherworldly."

She felt a reaction from him that matched her own. Surprise. Why was that? Izzi could read people, but she didn't purposely invade their privacy. She didn't get this kind of strong reaction unless the person was projecting.

What was it she felt from him? Shock?

Yes, that was it. He was shocked the word had slipped from his mouth. Typically, he was very much in control and rarely suffered a slip of the tongue.

Izzi Adams rattled him. Or was it

something more?

Without thinking, she reached over to put
her hand on his shoulder, and for a split
second, she saw herself as he saw her. Just
months shy of being eighteen, she was a
small young woman, barely over five feet
tall and probably weighing no more than a
hundred pounds.

Her hair was cut short, like a pixie, in
uneven layers, framing her face. White
with small streaks of silver, it gave her the
look of a fairy princess from a fantasy
tale.

Adding to the effect were her eyes.

They were mesmerizing and a bit
unsettling. He'd never seen that shade of
green. It reminded him of a bead on a
necklace his wife prized. While it looked
like a pearl, it displayed all the colors of
the spectrum, depending upon how the
light hit it, but no matter how strong or
weak the light, the color remained a pale
pearlescent that seemed magical.

Magical. That seemed to him a fitting
description for Izzi Adams.

She'd never been so flattered, or so flustered. She removed her hand from his shoulder. "You're a kind man, Agent Grant."

"It's true."

"Is it?"

"Yes." His expression changed, along with the subject. "You're young to already be a sophomore in college."

"Am I? As I understand it, a lot of people graduate high school early. Particularly those who aren't very social."

"You're not social?"

She laughed and looked out of the side window for a moment. "What do you think?"

"Well, you're in college, quite personable as far as I can tell, lovely and—"

"And unable to tell anyone about myself because if I do, I go from being the unusual girl with the white hair and strange eyes to the girl who watched her family die and nearly lost her eyes."

She looked at him and said, "Go ahead. Ask."

"I just want to know what happened. If you can tell it. I want to know what you saw, smelled, heard, and felt. Again, if you can talk about it."

She pulled her bottom lip up between her teeth for a few moments, her gaze seeking his and holding firm.

Leo could have sworn he heard a whisper in the car. No, it was coming from inside his head. Or was it?

Izzi reached over and took his hand. They both looked down at the same time, seeing her small white hand in his, the sharp contrast between skin tones and size so striking. It was strangely fitting in a way she couldn't describe. His gaze returned to hers, and she smiled.

"Have you ever heard of a viewer, Agent Grant?"

"Leo. And yes, why?"

"Because I am one."

"How do you know?"

"I've been examined more times than I can count, remember? Psychologists and psychiatrists find me of interest. I nearly lost my sight but recovered, and along with restored eyesight, new abilities manifested."

"I didn't read anything about this in your case history."

"Because it's not part of the case. And I can't take a chance on him knowing."

"Him? Him, who?"

"The person you're looking for."

"The Seven Bridges Killer?"

"Is that what you call him? Why?"

"I'm not at liberty to discuss certain aspects of our investigation."

"Of course not. You're here to ask questions, not provide answers."

"Sarcastic much?"

She couldn't help but smile. "A three-pointer for the short guy," she said, good-naturedly. "Sorry."

"My apology, Izzi. I'd love to be able to give you all the information I have, but I can't."

"I know. It's okay."

"Thank you."

"Where do you want me to start?"

"Don't you want coffee?"

"No, let's just sit here in your car, if that's okay."

"It's fine. Do you mind if I record this?"

"That's fine."

"I couldn't help noticing that stone you've been rubbing since you got into the car. Is there something special about it?"

"It's a worry stone."

"A worry stone? Where did you get it?"

Izzi offered the stone to him, which surprised her a little. As a rule, she hated for people to touch it. "My grandfather gave it to me when I went to live with him and my grandmother. This one is rose quartz, and my Pop carved it by hand. He taught me how to carve them. It's a time-consuming process."

"Why is it so hot? And it feels like it's vibrating. Is that normal?"

"It is when I've been holding it."

"Fascinating. It's pretty. Very smooth. What's the purpose?"

"From what I understand, rubbing the stone creates a

sense of relaxation and generates a sense of calmness." She gave him a slight smile. "Sort of like getting someone to talk about something familiar and comforting to put them at ease."

Leo chuckled and returned the stone to her. "I was sincerely interested."

"I don't doubt your sincerity or your methods. Now, ask your questions."

"If you're certain?"

"I am."

"Very well." Leo took a small digital recorder from his jacket pocket, turned it on, and held it up in front of him. "This is Special Agent Leo Grant. I am with Isabelle Adams at the University of North Carolina in Charlotte."

He recited the date and time, then set the recorder on the dashboard between himself and Isabelle.

"Miss Adams, what can you tell me about the murder of your mother and brother?"

"You mean aside from what I've told everyone else who has interviewed me?"

"Yes, is there anything other than what you've already given in previous statements? What can you tell me about that day?"

She leaned her head back, eyes focused on the ceiling of the car. "First, and for the record, if there is one, I truly despise that question. I hate being asked, and I hate being someone it happened to. That man..."

She turned her head and looked at Leo. "I don't think I'll ever stop being angry. Or sad. Not ever. He did such horrible things, caused my mother and brother such terrible pain. He's a monster. A psychopath.

"I didn't know he was there. We were in Donny's room, Donny and me. He was playing Mario on that old game console, and I was playing solitaire. My mother taught me and gave me a deck of cards.

"Donny didn't care about playing cards and didn't care that I did. He just liked having me in the room with him while he played that video game. He loved that game. Anyway, our dad wasn't due to be home for another day. He'd been gone a while this time. I heard my mother say on the phone that dad was picking up some extra trips so they could get her car fixed.

"The door opened, and my mother..." Izzi's gaze returned to the ceiling of the car.

She wasn't ready to tell anyone how she felt, then or

now. Maybe she never would be. It would take more trust than she could imagine to allow someone to hear her say what went on inside her, what she was made to feel.

It was a shame she couldn't tell Agent Grant what he wanted to know, but she had no reason to put that much trust in him. Maybe one day. Or maybe not.

If she made the mistake of truly opening up to someone, **he** would know, and the person she told might well be in danger.

She couldn't allow anyone else to be in peril from that monster, and that's how she thought of him as something whose soul was spawned in hell. So, she'd give Agent Grant as much as she could, without putting him in peril.

"God, the awful things he did. Her screams were— were agonized. I've never heard anything like that. I didn't want to hear or see. But he glued our eyes open, so we had to see.

"It seemed like he enjoyed the screams. He laughed. I still remember that sound. Laughing, laughing.

"Vomit kept rising up my throat, spewing out along with my screams and cries for him to stop. Mama kept pleading for him to stop, to let us go. He kept telling her to shut up and beat her more. But she wouldn't stop, so he used a big knife and a pair of pliers and cut her tongue out.

He shoved it in Donny's mouth, and Donny vomited all over the place. The man laughed even more and cut out Mama's eyes. He threw them at me. They landed right in front of me.

"I wanted to hurt him so bad. At first, I couldn't stop screaming, but then I realized that the screaming made him happy. I didn't want him to be happy. I wanted him to be dead. So, I stopped and told Donny to stop.

"It must have made him mad when we stopped screaming. Donny was just whimpering, and my mother was moaning and twisting on the floor, blind and bleeding. The man yelled at me. "You want to see what I'm going to do next?

"I didn't answer, and he grabbed Mama by the hair and started slamming her head into the floor. I screamed at him to stop and he did. "That's better," he said and sat on top of Mama. Then he used that big knife and stabbed her so hard her whole body jerked. He didn't pull the knife out, he just sawed and sawed and all the while these sounds came from her that..."

Izzi closed her eyes, trying to control her breath,

which had accelerated, along with her heart rate. "Finally, he tossed the knife aside and jammed his hand into her. He tugged and pulled, and blood went everywhere, and when his hand came free, something was in it. Something that more than filled his hand. He turned to face me and said, "Do you know what this is?"

"I couldn't have spoken even if I tried. He smiled, grabbed the knife, and moved over in front of me. "Your mother's heart. Look. It's the last thing you'll ever see."

Then he shoved her heart at my face, smeared it all over me, tossed it aside, and came at me with that knife. He cut me. My eyes. I've never felt that kind of pain. I heard the same sounds, the same screams coming from me that had come from my mother. I couldn't see."

She glanced at Leo and saw the compassion on his face and in his eyes. He reached out and put his hand on the side of her face and a sob caught in her throat. She felt his emotions, his empathy, and sincere regret for what had happened.

It weakened her without her even realizing it. She tilted her head just a fraction, pressing the side of her face ever so slightly against his big, warm hand. Sudden visions assailed her, completely took control. Her and Leo. Intimate moments.

Izzi couldn't control them, maybe she didn't want to. These weren't memories. They were visions of what was to come. God, was she projecting what she wanted, or was she seeing an actual future?

His sudden intake of breath snatched her back to reality. Unable to look at him, she blinked back tears and closed her eyes. "But I could hear. I could hear my brothers screams and moans and when he went silent, I knew it was my turn. But the silence got deeper and then I heard a whisper. "We're not done yet, you and me. I'll be back for you, Isabelle. Make no mistake. You're mine."

Oh shit. Izzi suddenly jerked away from him, unclenched her hands, opened the door, and looked out for a minute. She'd screwed up. She should never have told Agent Grant about what the murderer said.

She'd let the visions rattle her and screwed up.

"Is there anything you can tell me about him?" Leo asked. "Hair color? Skin color?"

"No. He wore black. All black. Black clothes and gloves and a black mask, the kind you see in kinky sex magazines. I couldn't even see what color his eyes were. I wish I could tell you what you want to hear, but I can't. I don't know." Right now, all she wanted was for this interview to come to an end. She didn't want to take the chance she'd slip up again.

"It's okay,"

Leo assured her. "Is there anything else you want to say?"

"Yes." She turned in her seat to face him. "He was wrong."

"About what?"

"About my mother's heart being the last thing I'd see."

"You saw something else?"

"Yes. I saw an angel. She was standing behind him, and she said not to be afraid.

"An angel. I – I'm sorry, but I don't believe in being disingenuous, so I must admit that I don't believe in angels. I do, however, understand that in extreme times of pain or fear, people can conjure up all manners of visions that feel very real to them."

"Yes, and I know you think I'm nuts, but that's okay. I know what I saw. She had white hair. Like me– like mine became. When my hair all fell out, I thought maybe God was mad at me for being alive when my mom and Donny weren't. Perhaps that's why my eyes didn't get better.

"Then, when I had the transplant surgery and could

see again, I saw that my hair was just like the angel's. I thought maybe I had died and didn't know it and I was an angel, too. But I hadn't died. I was still here, and my dad could barely stand to be in the same house with me. My grandparents looked at me like I was some creature, and I was alone. But, I sure as heck wasn't an angel."

"Well, you may not be an angel, but you're pretty as one." This time he reached out and took her hand. When he did, her gaze connected with his, and a current of energy seemed to bind them together, from their physical point of contact and from the connection of their eyes. It was strange and a bit disconcerting, but also quite interesting.

"You're kind, Agent Leo." A ghost of a smile tilted the corners of her mouth. "Maybe next time I see you, we can get that coffee. Or even better, a milkshake. I love milkshakes. Do you?"

"Yes, I do. But do you think there'll be a next time?"

Her smile vanished. "I know there will be."

His expression said he didn't believe her, but he was polite in his response. "Then it's a date."

"Is it?"

"Absolutely."

"All right then. I'll be seeing you, Special Agent Leo Sebastian Grant." She released his hand, grabbed her backpack from the floorboard where she'd tossed it, and slid out of the car.

Leo leaned over to better see her and smiled. "That will be my pleasure, Miss Isabelle Adams. Want me to take you back to where we met?"

"No, I'll walk. Safe journey."

With a wave, she turned and walked away. She could almost feel him watching her, but didn't turn around. Izzi had no doubt at all that she'd see him again. He was destined to be an important part of her life.

What she didn't know yet, was his importance one that eventually led to happiness?

Or more pain and loss.

With the way her life had been so far, she'd reluctantly have to bet on the latter.

.

.

Chapter Six

2020
Quantico, Virginia

As ridiculous as it seemed, Leo felt like he was walking the path of his past, accompanied by another. It was almost like Izzi was there with him, reliving the moments they shared as it replayed in his mind.

He dismissed the idea. Even had she known he was thinking of the past, she couldn't join him there. The past was done. It could be remembered and learned from, but that was it. Well, perhaps not. Right now, it seemed to have a powerful hold on him. Since there was still a bit of time before he and Galen reached their destination, Smithy's Bar, their hangout since they first met, Leo gave in and let the past claim him again.

2008
In Route to Quantico, Virginia

Leo spent the flight back to D.C. thinking about Izzi. What bothered him the most was the sudden attack of daydreams, visions, or imaginings–he wasn't sure what to label them– that had seized him.

Him and Izzi. She was older, stunning, with longer hair and a figure that was more womanly, not so waiflike, but still petite. They were intimate, and more than merely physical. He could feel her in his mind. They were lovers.

What was wrong with him to have had such imaginings? He was a good fifteen years older. Not old enough to be her father, but certainly too old to have such thoughts about a seventeen-year-old girl.

Only she wasn't seventeen in the visions. Still, it wasn't right and was most definitely out of character. Since the day he first saw Margaux, his wife, he'd not lusted after another woman. Leo was ashamed and even more troubled. He would have to give that serious thought.

Actually, he'd have to give everything about the time he spent with Isabelle Adams serious thought. He believed she'd been honest in what she said. He could detect a lie with ease, and she had not lied.

But, neither had she been entirely forthcoming.

She was hiding something, and he suspected it was something she'd not tell anyone because there was no one she could trust with that truth.

I'll always protect you, Izzi. Always.

He saw her sad smile, felt the touch of her hand on the side of his face. "As I will you."

What the hell? Leo jolted in his seat. Was he having some kind of psychotic episode? He'd never once in his life had a vision. Now, twice in one day, images conjured out of nothingness held sway over reality.

He needed to get a grip.

Perhaps she'd rattled him more than he wanted to admit. She couldn't know his middle name, and yet she did. But she couldn't have. Not even if she had called to verify his identity after they spoke on the phone when he called to request the interview.

"Then I'll be seeing you, Agent Leo Sebastian Grant."

There was no explanation.

"Maybe next time I see you, we can get that coffee. Or even better, a milkshake. I

love milkshakes. Do you?"

"Yes, I do.

But do you think there'll be a next time?"

Her smile vanished. "I know there will be."

How could she know?

Could she divine the future? Was she psychic? Leo had never been entirely convinced that anyone could see into the future.

Have you ever heard of a viewer?

He'd read reams of information on the topic of viewers. Remote viewing, an alleged paranormal ability that allowed a person to perceive a remote or hidden target without support of the senses, once held scientific interest and even attracted the attention of the CIA, as a possible means of spy-craft. Despite a variety of programs and millions of dollars, no usable intelligence data was produced.

No, he didn't believe remote viewing to be a dependable or even verifiable tool or ability. And that had nothing to do with her knowing they would meet again. Could she think of the term as something else? He wished he'd asked when she bought it up, then dismissed that line of thinking. He was about to dismiss the idea that she had any unusual ability at all when it popped back into his head again.

I'll be seeing you, Agent Leo Sebastian Grant.

Leo fished the miniature recorder from his pocket and stared at it. If he played this tape for his unit, questions would arise from the things she'd said. Questions that might lead the BAU to consider her worthy of additional interviews.

Why did something inside him balk at that notion? He realized with a good measure of surprise that he felt a strong need to protect her.

Was that because of his own daughter, Ayanna, was the same age now that Izzi had been when she witnessed the murders of her mother and brother?

It made Leo feel a bit ill to even consider something like that happening to his child. He'd gladly die for Ayanna, or her mother, Margaux. And he'd spend his life hunting down and killing whoever harmed either of them. They gave his life meaning, even when the road was a bit bumpy.

Like now. Margaux hated his job, and there were more times than he liked to remember when they'd fought about it. She wanted him to take a position in the private sector. With his education and credentials, he would find many doors that would open for him.

The problem was, Leo didn't want to leave the BAU. Margaux once said it was silly for him to think he was making a difference. Nonetheless, he did, and he hoped one day it would stop being a point of contention between them.

Until then, he tried to use his time off to do all the things Margaux wanted to do, to travel and experience new places. Those were the times when he saw her for the woman he'd fallen in love with. The woman who wanted to travel the world, see all there was to see, to view and touch structures she considered brilliant architecture and hopefully let them inspire her to create some of her own.

Sometimes Leo wondered why she'd fallen for him. He wasn't keen on travel and was far happier sharing a bottle of wine and helping prepare dinner than dining out in a fancy restaurant or breaking bread with Yak herders in a yurt.

Opposites attract. He smiled as he remembered his father speaking those words. They certainly applied to Leo and Margaux, and while their relationship might not be as smooth a sail as he'd like, the one thing they'd accomplished quite magnificently was Ayanna.

For that, he'd love Margaux forever and protect her and their daughter even at the cost of his own life.

That prompted a sad realization. Isabelle Adams had no one to fight for her. Her father was deceased, as were her grandparents. She was alone, without a champion.

That thought spurred an action that both shocked and disturbed him. Leo removed the tape from the recording device, pulled it loose from its housing, and quickly wadded it into a tangle, which he shoved into his jacket pocket.

No one would ever hear her words or know what she'd revealed in the interview. He'd relay information to his unit, but not all. There were things he'd keep to himself, things that need not go down on paper for someone else to see.

Chances were he'd never see her again, and that was probably for the best, but just this once, he'd be her protector, and without the tape, no one would ever know.

Not even her.

Eager for a distraction, Leo turned his thoughts to thoughts on the upcoming investigation and let that occupy him for the rest of the trip. He was the first one off the plane and headed down the ramp, reaching for his phone.

It rang the moment he turned it on. He dodged people disembarking from the plane and answered. "Grant."

"You back yet?"

Galen's voice was barely audible in all the noise of the people around Leo.

"Yeah, just got off the plane."

"Come in. There are developments."

"I promised Margaux—"

"Then you'll have to break that promise, buddy. Gib said to get here ASAP. All hands on deck. No exceptions."

"On my way."

Leo hurried to the parking deck and waited until he was in his car before calling his wife.

"On the ground?" she asked.

"I am. But I have to go to work. No exceptions. Gib called in the entire team."

"Of course, and we can't argue with the Great

Gibson Foster, can we?"

"Margaux, you know it had to be important for him to call in everyone this late. People's lives could be at stake."

"As you constantly remind me. What about the life of our marriage?"

"Sweetheart, you know I love you, and you know our life means everything to me. But one of us has to earn a living—"

"Oh, yeah, throw that up to me. I don't contribute."

"You know I don't feel that way. We both agreed it was important for Ayanna to have one parent at home until she was in school and—"

"Yeah, I know. Now that she is, I could get off my ass and do something."

Leo knew Margaux was projecting her own lack of self-worth onto him. It was a way for her to escape dealing with what bothered her. "Darling, I don't think that way at all. And I promise I'll get home as soon as I can, but this is—"

"Fine, whatever." The line went dead.

Leo thought about calling again but dismissed the impulse. She clearly wasn't in the mood to listen, and there was no benefit to either of them to get into another argument for which there was no solution.

As he navigated to the bottom of the parking deck, he turned his attention to the problems in his marriage.

He wasn't sure what it would take to bring him and Margaux back together. He supposed he could quit the BAU, but then he'd be giving up a career he loved, and to do what? Teach?

Maybe that would appeal to him one day, but not now. And even if he did, the money wasn't as good, and it wasn't as if she was working to help keep them afloat. That degree she'd almost earned had never been completed, and she'd come up with numerous excuses why she couldn't go back to finish.

Which circled him right back to where he'd started. Frustrated and without a clue how to make things better. Leo knew things couldn't go on indefinitely the way they were, but he simply didn't have answers, so he did what he did best when it came to such situations. He avoided it and buried himself in work.

Which, in Margaux's mind, made him the villain of their little play.

He pulled out of the parking deck and headed for

Quantico. Who knows, maybe she was right.

Leo met Marty on his way in.

"Everyone's in the conference room," Marty said, then paused to get a better grip on the stack of folders in his arm. He was listing to one side, thanks to all he carried and having the strap of a messenger bag, that was stuffed to overflowing, hanging on his shoulder.

"Give me that." Leo took the stack of folders.

"Thanks." Marty grabbed the strap of the messenger bag with both hands to take weight off his shoulder.

"What's up?" Leo asked as they started walking again.

"Murders. Three in three days. Same MO. The latest was yesterday, but we weren't notified until today after the M.E. finished examining the body and the state forensic lab finished."

"Where?"

"Arkansas. A co-worker showed up to give the victim a ride to work and discovered her dead. He called the police, who called in the state police, who called in the FBI field office in Jackson."

Marty stopped as Leo opened the conference room

door, then entered at a gesture from Leo.

"Good, you're here." Gib's acknowledgment cut short any more conversation.

Leo set the stack of folders on the table and rounded the table to take a seat between Galen and David.

Marty made himself busy, passing out folders. Leo leaned a little closer to Galen. "Are we going to see a fresh scene or have local P.D. stomped all over it?"

"Why? You think they'll be more careful than the last?"

"A man can hope."

Just then, Gib spoke up. "I'll make this short. I called you in for a briefing, but plans have changed. We're headed for Arkansas. If you don't have a go-bag, get home and get packed. Wheels up in two hours. If you have time before take-off, read the packet. I'll brief you on the flight. Go, people."

Gib's words had a dichotomous effect on Leo. On the one hand, the idea that they might get to the scene before possible evidence was destroyed made him eager to get there. That excitement conflicted with the dread of facing Margaux and telling her he would be away for a few days. He wished he didn't have to go home and pack a bag.

It would be a fight and not one he wanted to have. But chances were, he'd start this trip with a knot in his gut that was wound tight around growing resentment and a genuine inability to understand why Margaux had stopped supporting him in his goals and stopped pursuing her own.

It would take a hell of a lot more than a good investigator to figure that out.

The Present

Leo shoved aside thoughts of the past and reached up to rub his fingertips over his eyes. He wondered if he looked half as tired as he felt.

"Remember when you convinced Gib to go see her?" Galen broke the silence. "To consider her as a civilian consultant?"

"Of course, I remember. Why ask?"

"You never told anyone exactly why you were convinced she was psychic. Aside from her knowing your middle name even though you never told her."

"I thought you wanted to wait until we got to Smithy's," Leo pointed out.

"Is it that hard to talk about?"

"No. Yes. Bloody hell, G, you know that time is still

a thorn in my side. Correction, in Margaux's side. She'll never give up asking who the woman was I had an affair with, and I'll never stop hiding that truth from her."

"Have you ever asked yourself why?"

"I don't have to ask." Leo looked at his partner. "Izzi isn't normal, and I don't say that in a disparaging manner. Margaux would never understand my attraction to her, and the difference in age would always have her thinking I see her as old in comparison."

"I can see that," Galen conceded. "So back to Miss Adams and her psychic skills."

"I'll be honest. I always knew there was something different about her. But it wasn't until that Soccer Mom killing spree that I realized she was, in fact, genuinely psychic."

"Yeah, I remember. That damn case had us going for months, and the body count kept climbing. I thought Gib was going to lose his mind. Then you opened your mouth and suggested we bring in a psychic consultant."

He chuckled, and after a moment, so did Leo. "Remember Marty's face when I said it was Isabelle Adams?"

This time it wasn't a chuckle but a full-blown laugh. Within moments both men were nearly crying from laughter. Galen wiped his eyes and blew out a breath. "If ever the expression "deer in the headlights" was applicable, it was that moment. I didn't know until right then that he knew about you and Isabelle."

"Neither did I," Leo admitted. "Smarty Marty was quite observant. He saw me leaving with Izzi after that lecture at UNCC, and I guess he put the pieces together as time went along."

"He was off the chart brilliant and, in the end, a brave man. I still miss him."

"As do I,"

Leo agreed. Marty's replacement and the one who followed were smart and capable, but none of them had what Marty had possessed. Innocent brilliance. He was naive about the concepts of hatred and rage, and it always shocked him that people could be so horrible. He wanted to stop them so they could be helped.

That was what got him killed. His sincere desire to help. Leo felt it was one of life's unfairness, that someone with Marty's goodness should be taken so young while evil doers enjoyed long lives.

"Which brings us back to why you wanted Miss Adams involved."

"Oh yes."

Leo wasn't surprised that Galen had circled back to his original topic. He was, as the American saying went, *like a dog with a bone* when he got something stuck in his mind. He'd mentally chew on it until he either figured it out or the problem went away.

"Well, let's see. We'd been seeing one another for almost six months. I made an excuse for having to be away while Margaux's parents were in town and planned on spending a long weekend with Izzi.

"Then we were handed the Seven Bridges and the Soccer Mom cases all at once. I had to cancel, and it was two weeks before I got back to North Carolina to see her. I couldn't get a flight, so I drove down as soon as Gib cut us loose.

"I was exhausted by the time I arrived. We couldn't catch a break in either case, Gib was getting pressure from above, and we were all running about like a pack of dogs trying to get the scent of the fox."

"Spoken like a Brit, but you're right. It was pretty bad."

"It was and must have shown on my face because

Izzi took one look at me, ordered me to take a seat at the table, poured me a drink, and then cooked me a meal. Once I'd eaten, she poured me another drink and said, "Okay, talk to me."

"I didn't talk to her about work. I never had discussed or revealed anything about the cases we worked. Not until that moment. She sat at the table, playing solitaire with a deck of cards that were so old and worn you couldn't even shuffle them. I must have bought her fifty new packs because she was always playing solitaire, but she never opened them. She still played with that worn-out deck. Finally, I gave up.

"Anyway, this night, she sat there, playing without really looking at the cards. Her focus was on me. Early in our relationship, the level of concentration in her gaze made me uncomfortable. I'd grown beyond it. Or thought I had.

"That night, her focus was eerie. I can't tell you why it felt that way, it just did. Her gaze was unwavering, laser-beam targeted, and it made me uneasy. But I finished telling her about the cases and our problems.

"She nodded, gathered up her cards, mixed them up, and then laid three cards on the table, all face down. "So, what keeps you from finding these people. These Unsubs?"

"Which ones?"

"The Soccer Mom Killer?"

"Why that one and not the other? The Seven Bridges Killer."

"You know. I don't want to talk about the other." She cut a quick look at him.

"Fine," Leo agreed. "We won't discuss that case. Are you sure you want to talk about the Soccer Mom Killer?

"Yes. What's keeping you from finding him or her?"

"A starting point. A clue. Something, anything that points a direction."

Leo paused and loosened his necktie. "She nodded and turned over a card. When she looked up at me, I nearly dropped my glass, but she didn't seem to notice, or if she did, she didn't comment. Her eyes were white. It was creepy."

"They'd never be afraid of him," she said. "That's why he chooses them. "

"I don't mind telling you I experienced a jolt of discomfort, more than a bit of unease.

Not entirely from her words, but the manner in

which she spoke them. So matter of fact, as if she were reciting weather statistics from the past week. And the fact that her eyes were entirely white."

"White, like the pale green faded?" Galen interrupted.

"No, as in all white. No iris color at all. Just a sea of white with a black pupil. It was unnatural and a bit frightening, but I choked back my discomfort, wanting to hear more.

"What do you mean?" I asked her.

"She shrugged and turned over another card. "Just what I said. They'd never think of being afraid of him. He's what they dream their little boys will be."

"So, how old is this guy? Is he a coach or a teacher? How does he find them?

"Izzi turned over another card but never looked at it. Her attention was on me as she spoke. "So handsome, smart, and talented. He's every mother's dream, and some mothers' secret little fantasy."

"Secret fantasy?"

"Yes." She smiled. "The kind of boys they all coveted in their youth, the one who could have any girl, the one they thought would become someone famous and sought after. The kind they see now and masturbate, thinking of how they'd seduce him. He's the kind they see photos of online and save to their computers, in a file labeled recipes or decorating tips, something their husbands will never open."

Then she took the top card from the stack on the table and turned it face up – the three of hearts.

"He has three more to kill," she said. "Three more hearts to give her."

"Give who?"

"The one who demands he brings her proof of his love."

"You're saying he's doing this for a woman?"

"Not a woman." She plucked another card from the deck and turned it face up, this time the Queen of Spades. "His queen."

"A breath later, she blinked, and her eyes were normal. Well, normal for her. She stared at me for a moment, then gathered up her cards. "I'm tired."

"With that, she left the room. I sat there for a long time, not sure what to think and certainly not what to say.

What had just happened? Finally, I went into the bedroom, undressed, and got into bed with her. She rolled over, put her head on my shoulder, and her arm across my chest. I told myself to forget it. Maybe she was just messing with me. But that didn't make sense, and it was out of character.

"Still, I didn't know how to talk to her about it. I suppose it rattled me more than I was willing to admit. And because of that, I made a point *not* to mention it."

"So that's it," Galen said and hammered his hand on the steering wheel. "How could I have not seen it?"

"What are you talking about?"

"The pictures on the computer," Galen said. "There was another murder. You and I were in the victim's room. Her laptop was sitting on the makeup table. You made a beeline for it. There was no password required. There was, however, a folder labeled recipes, and inside it were photos of men the woman had saved from places she visited online.

"All blonde and blue-eyed, dressed either in what was considered a preppy fashion for the time, or a soccer uniform."

Galen cut a look at Leo. "She profiled the killer for us and led us straight to the photos. When I asked what made you think of looking in a recipe folder, you had no answer. But a week later, we caught the guy, and sure enough, he was killing for his queen. For his batshit crazy mother. Talk about a dangerously insane family."

"That's an understatement," Leo was quick to agree. The mother, as it turned out, was the mastermind, the one who planned the murders, and her son just carried them out. They had an unnatural relationship that made Leo feel dirty to consider and made him wonder how such an incestuous and criminal relationship began.

"And when the next case was handed to us, you went to Gib and asked that he hire Isabelle Adams as a civilian consultant," Galen brought Leo back on track. "Not because of her degree, but because you believed her psychic ability would lead us to the Seven Bridges Killer, and we could put to bed a case no one had been able to solve in over a decade."

There was silence when Galen finished speaking, and that silence lasted until they pulled into the parking lot of the bar. At nearly one in the morning, there weren't many cars in the lot, and there wouldn't be many people inside. Just the career drunks, who wouldn't leave until they had no choice and the people who'd lost control of their lives and didn't know where else to go.

Galen turned off the engine and looked at Leo. "Do you ever wish you hadn't asked Gib to bring her in?"

"Every day, my friend."

"Then why didn't you stop him from making the same mistake again?"

Leo shook his head. "Because this time it wasn't my mistake to make. It was his."

Galen nodded. "Then God help us all, buddy. We lost Marty in 2010 and almost lost you in 2012, and then Gib nearly bit the dust a little over a year ago. Isabelle Adams might be psychic, but as far as I can see, she's also bad luck. I don't know about you, but I don't want to end up in a drawer in the morgue because she led us down a path we shouldn't travel."

"She'd never do anything to intentionally hurt any of us, Galen. You know that as well as the rest of us."

"Maybe, but it isn't always ill intentions that get people killed, my friend. I'm just not sure her hunches or psychic insights, whatever you want to call them, are worth the loss of a member of our team.

"I hear you, G, but Gib calls the shots. Besides, he might not even talk her into it. She was adamant about being done with it, and whether you like the woman or not, you know she loves him. She never left his bedside the entire time he was in the coma. She sat there day and night, talking to him, holding his hand."

"And then gave him the boot once he was on his feet again. That's a strange kind of love, buddy. A damn strange kind."

"Maybe," Leo said and opened his door. "But love nonetheless."

He got out and looked at Galen across the top of the car. "And again, not our call."

"So, how do we play this, if she comes back?"

"By the book," Leo answered, meaning that with all sincerity. This time feelings could not come into play. "This time, it has to be by the book. For all of us."

What he didn't add was something that had been eating at him ever since Gib said he was going to try and convince Izzi to come back. Leo couldn't say it aloud, but he feared that if they didn't go by the book, and keep it strictly professional, the monster she once told him she feared, would somehow zero in on her.

And Izzi would die.

No matter how much physical or emotional distance stood between them now, Leo couldn't bear the thought of that. He knew they weren't meant for one another. But she still owned a piece of his heart, and he wasn't ready for that piece to be shattered.

Cabarrus County, North Carolina

Izzi's mind would give her no peace. Memories assailed her, demanding attention. At present she was caught in a remembrance of the day she met Leo Grant. It was 2005 and she was a sophomore at the University of North Carolina...

Why had meeting Leo Grant caused her to be taken with thoughts of her past and all its terror and pain? She'd left his car ten minutes ago but felt she was still trapped by his presence. Her pace increased until she was running. What was he meant to be to her? She wasn't sure she wanted to know. She just wanted to be somewhere safe, somewhere private.

Her dorm room. She ran until her breath was ragged, bolted up the stairs and into her room. Izzi locked the door, hurried to the window and opened it wide. She stood there for several minutes, feeling the fresh air in her face and letting the familiar sounds from the dormitory soothe her.

Meeting with Leo Grant had delivered unexpected surprises, and she needed time to assimilate and organize all the images that'd flooded her mind. She knew better than to try and force it. Things would make sense on their own when her mind finished processing. Until then, the best thing she could do was busy her brain with something else.

The something else that pressed at her wasn't what she wanted in her mind. Speaking with Leo had resurrected old terrors and pains, along with old questions.

Isabelle hadn't been entirely honest with Leo.

There were things she couldn't bring herself to say, couldn't force the words from her lips.

How, once she was bound, the killer had stroked her face, whispered to her that she was his special girl.

Izzi would rather have her tongue cut out than to tell anyone about that, or about the other things.

Things the doctors had not thought to look for when they examined her. The demon thought he'd made her his that day.

He was wrong. She'd never be his anything, other than his slayer if given the opportunity. She prayed God would grant her the chance to fill that vital role. Izzi wasn't a religious person, but she firmly believed that evil was real, and there had to be warriors willing to fight it. Destroy it. She wanted desperately to be the warrior who vanquished this monster.

No, she'd not tell anyone about those things. She'd

spent the better part of her life wishing she could forget them. There were things about that day she couldn't remember, gaps in her memory. As much as she wanted to forget what she did remember about that day, she'd never been able to stop trying to fill in the blanks. Why was it such an obsession?

Would it help her to destroy the monster if she remembered?

When she was fourteen, she realized that until she filled in the missing time, she would never find real peace or be able to move on. The trouble was, she didn't know how to look for the missing pieces to her gruesome puzzle. There was no one alive who could help her.

No one but him.

She wasn't ready to face him and would continue to hide from him for now. One day she'd be strong enough to take him on, and then she'd open a door in her walls. She knew he'd sense it and he'd call to her.

Isabelle had no clue if she'd survive that encounter, but sometimes that didn't matter. What did matter was getting to the truth. After that, she supposed it was up to fate. Or perhaps it was a decision left to God.

To decide whether she lived, or if it was her destiny

to destroy the monster in the dark.

Hours passed and the room began to lighten, signaling the coming of dawn. Izzi felt Gib's slow breathing against her back and the touch of his warm hand on her hip. *Please, God, if you're real, please don't let him be hurt again. Don't let any of them be hurt by the monster who stalks me. If my blood will stop him from killing more innocents, then let him have me.*

But if my blood won't appease him, then give me the power to destroy him. Once and for all. If it's a sin to put an end to this kind of evil, then place that sin on me and judge me for it. Just please, don't let anything happen to the people I love. Please.

It wasn't lost on her that her plea today was the same as what she'd prayed for twelve years ago and twenty-two years ago. To destroy the monster who'd taken her family from her. To end his evil and keep him from taking more lives.

Until this moment, she hadn't wanted to admit how much she wanted that or how much of her courage she'd lost. Seeing Gib nearly die from being stabbed by the monster, watching him fight for life and then hang in the gray place, that space between life and death for almost a month, had shattered her. She was sure she'd never survive that kind of pain if she had to go through it again.

Now, she made up her mind that wouldn't happen. She'd find the strength and courage, and she'd armor herself for battle. Her monster wanted one thing. Her. So, if she couldn't help the BAU find and stop him, then she'd give herself to him, and pray the angels were on her side.

Because one way or the other, this time, only one of them would walk away.

behind the
ROCKNG
HORSE

PART 2

"Hell is empty – all the devils are here."

William Shakespeare

Chapter Seven

Izzi leaned against the door with her arm propped up, holding loosely to the *oh-shit* handle as she called it, mounted just above the door. Her head rested against her arm, and sunglasses hid her eyes.

She'd been quiet ever since they left her home and spent the first two hours going over everything the FBI had on the last Seven Bridges killings. Gib had called the BAU and asked to have it sent to his iPad and gave it to her as soon as they were on the road. He wondered if she was having second thoughts about her decision to take the consulting position with the BAU.

"No." Her soft voice broke the silence.

"No, what?"

"No, I'm not thinking of backing out. After reading

the file and looking at the evidence and forensic reports, I think this crime is … different. He's too smart to make these mistakes, so either it isn't him or…"

She turned to look at Gib. "Or he's up to something new."

"Meaning?"

"I'm not sure yet. But this is not the same at all."

"Exactly what Galen and Leo have been saying."

"And you? What do you think?"

"I'm not sure yet."

"Smart answer."

She turned away again, and there was another half hour of silence. Gib loosened his necktie and unbuttoned the top button of his shirt, then cranked the AC up a notch. He wanted to ask what she was thinking, but didn't want her to feel he was pushing so his kept his silence.

A few more minutes passed before she spoke again. "The other case – the Cheerleader Killer?"

"What about it?"

"Why target cheerleaders?"

"That's the question, isn't it?"

"It is. Are we going to the scene of the last killing?"

"Actually, we're scheduled to leave this evening to visit both crime scenes."

"Good."

"Good?" He was surprised by that response. Izzi didn't typically want to view a crime scene and he understood her reasons. She didn't just see the aftermath of what had happened. All too often she saw a mental replay of the events, or felt the residual pain and terror. He was pretty sure that if he had her abilities, he'd want to steer clear of crime scenes as well.

"Yes." She nodded. "Is the entire team going?"

"Yes, as always."

"And who will I answer to?"

"Me."

"You think that's smart?"

"You don't?"

For the first time since he arrived at her home, her mood lightened, and the Izzi he knew and loved emerged. "Well, you know how I get about good-looking men in power. I mean, I'll do my best to keep to the yes sir and no sir, but you might want to keep your distance. Just in case … you know, I get overpowered by that air of command."

Gib smirked. "Smartass."

"I have my moments," she agreed lightheartedly, then grew somber. "Seriously, are you certain this isn't going to be an issue for Leo or G? They have seniority, and I don't want to step on any toes with my insights – or lack thereof."

"That won't be an issue."

"I hope not."

"Why would you think it might?"

Izzi shrugged. "I don't know. With Leo, it probably wouldn't be. He'd tell me straight up if I overstepped. But Galen? I guess I just never quite got the hang of being completely at ease around him. He's brilliant, insightful, and methodical, and I admire that, but he's so…"

"So what?" Gib asked when she left the thought unspoken.

She cut him a look over the top of her glasses. "Smoking hot and aware of it."

"Seriously?" That came as a shock.

"Oh, come on, you'd have to be blind not to realize that. He's incredibly handsome and very charismatic and seductive. I've paid a lot of attention to how women respond to him."

"Which is?"

"Well, first they're a bit star-struck over his looks. It's like coming face-to-face with a movie star and you know what I mean. I bet he had a lot of women wanting to be his Thelma or Louise when he was younger, and his looks didn't fade as he aged. He's one of those men who is always going to stand out because of his physical appearance.

"Then there's that smile he gives them like he just got his first look at what just might prove to be the ruling passion in his life. That figuratively knocks women off their feet. By the time he speaks to them in that low, *this is just between the two of us* voice, he has them – hook, line, and sinker. He could ask them to jump off a building, and they'd be damned tempted."

Gib chuckled. "I never knew you'd given Galen so much thought."

"I give *everyone* thought."

"So, this analysis – does it hold true for you as well?"

"No, but that's because I know that 90 percent of his charm is a tool, just like your ability to hear the space between people's words and dig beneath what they say, or Leo's skill in discerning whether someone is telling the truth. G's one of the smartest people I've ever met, and sure, he has a new woman every week, but I get the feeling he's a lonely person because no matter how crazy a woman is about him, he doesn't feel the same."

"You mean he doesn't fall in love?"

"Not now. Maybe once. Sometimes it feels like he lost the girl he loved or never told her or … I don't know exactly. Once, I thought perhaps he's gay, but in observing him when Leo and I would go out with him, I quickly dropped that hypothesis. Men come onto him, but he clearly isn't interested. Was he ever married or engaged?"

"You never asked him?" Gib cut a look at her.

"No, I didn't feel like it was my place. Besides, the times I've interacted with him were either about a case or in a social setting with other people. When it was related to a case, I paid attention to his insights, and when it was social, I just enjoyed his sense of humor and the fact that he's a great dancer and likes to have fun. But back to my question."

"He's never been married or engaged that I'm aware," Gib replied and then added, "Perhaps it has something to do with how he grew up. He lost his mother at an early age. Seven, I think. His father was in sales and traveled a lot, so he spent a good deal of time alone. His father's sister, who was older and unmarried, cared for him when his father was gone. She died the summer after Galen graduated high school. He was alone after that."

"Sounds like a lonely life." Izzi knew how that felt, and for the first time since she'd become acquainted with the man, she felt a common bond.

"Why the sudden interest in Galen?" Gib asked. "In all the years since you met him, you're just now curious?"

Izzi laughed. "No. I was always curious. I just kept it to myself and thought if I kept watching, I'd eventually figure him out. I can't say I ever really did."

"You mean you can't read him?"

"Some. Mostly surface stuff, like the burger gave him indigestion, or he hated the movie he went to the night before, or once that the woman he went out with smelled like fried chicken. Even her hair."

Gib laughed. "Profound impressions for sure."

"Oh yeah, no doubt. But the point is, he's one of those people who're pretty shut down emotionally. I guess maybe it does stem from childhood. I'm living proof that childhood can screw a person up."

"I don't think you're screwed up."

Izzi blew a raspberry in derision. "Liar. You know I am. I'm just a highly functional screwed up person. But all that... stuff...the fear and pain and memories I don't want ...it's all there, tormenting me when my mind gets quiet."

Gib reached for her hand. "I know, but you're stronger than all of it, and you don't let it control you."

"Like I said, highly functional screw up."

"If that's how you choose to label it, although I disagree. Still, it did seem there were times when it wasn't so bad."

"Because of you." She gave his hand a squeeze and admitted something she'd never said aloud. "When I'm with you, it's easier to keep the monsters at bay, or at least easier to be brave and sneer at them in the darkness. I know you'd die to save me, and I would for you."

This time when Gib looked at her, there was no smile on his face. "Iz, there's something I need to say to you. Something you wouldn't allow me to say before, and I'm asking that you give me that chance now."

She already knew what he wanted to say, and she wasn't sure she wanted him to say it, but she owed it to him to listen, so she nodded.

"Thank you. I know I would have died if you hadn't stepped in, offered yourself to him if he let me live. I never got the chance to thank you for saving me. Not properly. Hell, I don't even remember anything after you shot at him. Not until I woke up to be told I'd lost two months of my life being in a coma.

"No." He ran his left hand over his beard. "That's not true. I do remember things, but I don't know how much was real since I was unconscious."

"What do you remember?"

"You. Your hand holding mine, you stroking my face or rubbing my arm. Talking to me, telling me how much you needed me and how I needed to come back. I wanted to. I wanted to tell you how thankful I was and how incredibly brave you were. After being

139

his prisoner for nearly three months, to offer to go back into that cage..."

"Stop. Seriously, pull over Gib. There, at that next exit."

He did, and once he'd exited off the highway, he turned into the lot of a convenience store and parked. "Okay, what's wrong? If it's me saying–"

"No. I mean, yes. No, wait." Izzi held up one hand. "First, you never *ever* have to thank me for that. It was every bit as much for me as for you. There are things I can live with, things I can live without, and things I can endure. You *not* being part of my world isn't on either list. I'd rather have died than lived without you, so don't make me a hero.

"And you have to have figured it out a long time ago – particularly when he had me locked up. He's not ready to kill me. He might not ever be. As crazy as it sounds, I think he sees me as *his* creation. If *he* hadn't killed my family, if *he* hadn't cut my eyes, then I may not have ended up with–with an unusual physical appearance that sets me apart from others, along with extra senses. He sees himself as Dr. Frankenstein and me as his creation."

She still couldn't bring herself to confess the complete truth of what had transpired the night her mother and brother were murdered. Izzi wasn't sure she'd ever be able to force those words from her lips. If she did, she feared she'd make his taunt a reality.

You're mine, Isabelle. My special girl, my one true love.

Izzi shook those thoughts away and continued with what she could say. "In his sick and twisted way, he loves me, and I'm starting to think what he'd like is for me to succumb to him–to his ways and become… I don't know, his cheerleader or acolyte.

"He wants me to love him.

"And that's the one thing I won't do. I hate him, and I fully intend to end him. But I'll play my own game and fool him if I can, whatever it takes to get me face-to-face with him when the time is right. I want to look him in the eyes, tear the mask from his face, and see him for who he is.

"But that's not the point – so let me make this clear. You owe me nothing. You pulled me from that cage, from that dank basement where I thought I'd spend the rest of my life. But you heard me. You heard me calling to you and you came for me, even when it wasn't sanctioned and even when you knew you might be killed. So, if there's a hero in our tale, Gib, it's you, and if you're smart, you won't argue with me on this."

He looked at her for a long time, then shook his head and smiled. "Damn it all, Iz, if you're not the most confounding woman I've ever met."

"Yes, I am. I admit it. But you love me, and together we're going to trap monsters and make the world a safer place. Right, Mr. Special Agent in Charge?"

"Right, Dr. Adams. So, can I get back on the road?"

"Absolutely."

Once they were back on the highway, he cut a look at her. "Okay, let's go back to the Cheerleader Killer and what you said."

"Why cheerleaders, you mean?" She looked out of the side window. "I'm sure you all have looked at it six ways from Sunday. Tell me the profile the team came up with."

"That's just it. We haven't. Nothing fits. What would make a man want to kill cheerleaders for professional sports teams? We looked at all the possibilities. Was he involved with one and dumped? Did he get rejected when he made an advance on a cheerleader? Was someone he loved mistreated by a cheerleader? Did his girl try out and not make the cut? We made a list of every possibility we could think of and can't make any of the dots connect."

She turned the iPad on and reassessed the information. For an hour, neither of them spoke. Then she looked over at him. "You're right, it doesn't make sense. There's nothing that connects these women aside from the fact they're cheerleaders for a professional sports team – football and now basketball. What connects those two sports?"

"I wish I knew. Hopefully, when we visit the last scene, we'll see something everyone else missed."

She nodded and set the tablet aside again. "Can we stop at your house so I can change before we go to the Center?"

"You don't like what you're wearing?"

"It's not the impression I want to make if you don't mind."

"Then what impression do you want to make on people who already know you?"

"That today's Izzi might still be a little *woo woo*, a bit bohemian, and a lot outspoken, but she also holds two doctorates, teaches top law enforcement professionals, and is quite serious about the work at hand."

"I don't think they've forgotten your qualifications, Iz."

"Maybe, but you have to admit that my appearance has a strange effect on people. They tend to forget what I know and focus on my looks. I expect it from strangers and often use it to my advantage. I don't want it to always be that way with the people on your team, and when I worked as a consultant before, I felt most of them never got beyond my appearance.

"So, I decided I would change things a bit, and now when I lecture or work with law enforcement, I dress in a kind of a modified professional style. It gets immediate attention, but also allows people to move past appearance and accept me on a more mainstream level."

Gib chuckled and then grinned at her. "I can't wait to see what that looks like."

She returned the smile. "Smartass."

Suddenly it felt good to be there, preparing to work with him, and seeing the smile reach his eyes. She'd forgotten how much that fortified her spirit. She'd not forgotten that she loved him, but when he smiled that way...

The romantic side of her nature that she kept hidden gave a silent little sigh. When he smiled that way, it was hard not to fall *in* love with him all over again.

Chapter Eight

He raised his face to the sun, closed his eyes, and smiled at the feel of golden light on his skin.

Today was a pivotal day. Today marked the beginning of a change in more than merely his life. Today, the die was cast. There was no going back for any of them. Not that he wanted to go back. He had been working toward this day for years.

To his disappointment, manipulating the BAU had been far less of a challenge than he'd imagined. Gibson Foster, the Special Agent in Charge, had done exactly as hoped. He'd gone straight to Isabelle.

Ah, Isabelle.

Longing filled him at the thought of her. How long would he let her cling to her illusions, to believe she could turn her back on him, keep him from sensing her presence? She'd put so much effort into shutting him out. He felt a certain amount of pride in her limited success.

She was quite remarkable.

But not yet perfect.

She could be. Would be. As soon as she was his to keep forever.

His eyes opened as need clutched painfully, shortening his breath and making him ache. Sometimes waiting was excruciating; the need for her was so great. It had started to become too much to bear. He'd waited long enough. The time had come for him to finally claim what was his.

It was time for her to remember and understand that she belonged to him.

The memory of their meeting took control, sweeping him back in time. With a sigh, he allowed himself to be taken by the memory. He sank down onto the warm planks of wood of the boat dock that stretched out into the small cove of still water, closed his eyes, and in the space of a heartbeat was there.

Dust motes danced in the night breeze, illuminated like glowing dots as the moonlight from the window slanted across the room, casting it in stark contrasts of light and shadow. In the light of day, this room would be nothing more than a child's bedroom.

Tonight, it was hallowed ground, consecrated in blood and tears, in pleas for mercy that were ignored, screams for compassion that were disregarded. It was a place of learning for him, only the third time he'd been allowed to participate. A rite of passage and one he was determined to not only live up to but to prove himself ready for a more active role.

The children on the floor struggled in vain as their mother was brutalized. He could feel their fear and desperation to escape as he knelt with one knee on the boy's back, and his hands tightened into fists in the child's hair.

The boy showed far more fear than the girl. He sobbed, wet his pants, and pleaded for his life. The girl screamed, but it was as much in anger as fear. She shouted at his mentor to stop beating her mother's head into the floor. He smiled and complied.

Then he killed her mother. Stabbed her in the chest and cut her heart from her body as she screamed in agony. The sounds that emerged from her lips were inhuman. No, sacrosanct. Such sublime torment. It gave him an erection, and for a moment, he considered ripping the child's pants off and stabbing inside his tender flesh.

But he'd not been given permission to do anything but observe. So, he remained silent and watchful. Finally, his mentor tossed the knife aside and jammed his hand into the woman. He tugged and pulled, and blood went everywhere, and when his hand came free, something was in it. Something that more than filled his hand. He turned to look at the children and said, "Do you know what this is?"

The boy whimpered and soiled himself again. The girl was silent and still, even when he picked up the discarded knife and moved across the room. He kicked aside the rocking horse, that flimsy bit of wood the foolish children thought would hide them. Then he knelt in front of us. I yanked hard on the boy's hair, bending him backward so that my mentor's hands were directly in front of them.

He smiled and spoke to the girl. "Your mother's heart. Look. It's the last thing you'll ever see."

It was a moment he wished he could encase in resin, like the flowers you see in a trinket shop, forever preserved. He wanted to be the master. Wanted to know the ecstasy as the mentor shoved the woman's heart against the little girl's face, smearing it all over her.

He watched with every mounting excitement as his mentor quickly struck out with the knife.

Blood blossomed from the boy's throat.

For a few seconds, there were gurgling sounds that erupted from him. His body spasmed several times and then went still.

"I will kill you!" the girl screamed and struggled

The mentor laughed and gave an order. "Hold her very still."

There was no hesitation in obeying. Once she was imprisoned with hands on either side of her head, pulling it back even more, he started with the knife. How precise he was. One diagonal cut across each of her eyes. It was a thing of beauty, a moment so perfect, it was an honor to bear witness.

Then he smiled and stood. "I'll leave you to finish up here. End her and meet me outside."

What elation.

The mentor was going to allow him to participate. This was the moment he'd waited for his entire life. He stood and jerked the girl to her feet.

Thanks to the ropes binding her hands behind her, and holding her ankles in a crossed position, she was in no position to fight.

What happened next was to be the moment that changed his life forever. The part of him that was the strongest, turned her toward the light, revealing the paleness of her skin, so white beneath the blood from her mother's heart, and her own blood that poured from her once warm-brown eyes. Her breath was fast, and when he put a hand on her chest, he could feel the rapid pounding of her heart.

He knew she was afraid, yet she didn't scream. "Go ahead. Kill me."

That's when he realized. He didn't want her dead. He wanted her. So rather than finish what the mentor had started, for the first time ever, an act of disobedience was enacted. He leaned in close to her ear. "What's your name?"

"Isabelle."

"Isabelle." He liked the taste of her name on his lips, the feel of it. "You're mine. Do you understand that? I can kill you, or I can let you live. It's up to you. What do you want, Isabelle?"

"To kill you."

That delighted him.

If she lusted for his blood, then she could be taught to lust for the blood of others. He could become a master.

That had been his goal for years.

She would help him become what he desired.

"Listen to me, Isabelle. I'm going to let you live. But only if you do exactly what I tell you. Do you understand?"

Her nod was enough.

He pulled back and spoke softly.

"Open your mouth."

He was honestly surprised when she complied, but very excited. He opened his own mouth and extended his tongue and slowly kissed her. She didn't move, didn't protest or flinch as he put his tongue in her mouth.

It was divine. So much that he wanted more. She didn't fight him as he ripped away her clothing. She was so young, far from becoming a woman. Still, he wanted to be her first and so he took her, finding delight in her pain. When he ejaculated, he clutched her to him.

"You're mine now, Isabelle. My special girl, my one true love. Do you understand?"

"No."

"You will. Listen to me. I'm going to leave, and you're going to forget. There was a man here. A man all in black. Just one man. Do you understand."

"No."

He repeated it.

"If you remember it any other way, we'll come back. And we'll do to your daddy what we did to your mommy. We'll do it to anyone and everyone you care about. Do you understand now?"

There was a long moment before she answered. "Yes."

"Tell me what happened here, Isabelle?"

"A man was here. He did this. A man in black."

"Very good." He kissed her again, happy that she didn't fight it. "I'll see you again, Isabelle. When the time is right, I'll come for you."

She nodded, and he shoved her back down on the floor. "Don't make a sound or move."

There was no response.

He snapped back to the present. She'd kept her word. She never told anyone about him being there. Was that because she knew in her heart she belonged to him, or had she blocked out all memory of him?

He'd never gotten an answer to that question. Not even when he had her locked in the cage.

But he would. Very soon, he would.

Quantico, Virginia

Galen refilled his coffee cup and walked over to where Leo stood at the conference table, looking over Fiona Metcalf's shoulder, at the laptop sitting on the table in front of her. Fiona had eighteen years in with the Bureau, fifteen with the BAU as a criminal profiler, and had earned a reputation as one of the best.

"Crime scene photos?" Galen asked.

"Yes." She cut a look over her shoulder at him. "The latest Cheerleader shooting. Whoever this shooter is, he's good."

"How good?"

"Military-trained-good would be my guess. Say, has anyone heard from Gib?"

"I talked to him about twenty minutes ago," Leo replied. "He said they were on their way in."

That statement drew the attention of everyone in the room. Tamara Baker, a twenty-seven-year-old MIT graduate, specializing in data analysis and a top

154

researcher, got up from where she sat across the room at one of the consoles and walked over to the table. "So, is he bringing the consultant?"

"And is she a genuine psychic?" Dennis Brock, the youngest member of the team at twenty-six, asked.

"She holds two doctorates. Once in criminal psychology and another in parapsychology," Leo answered the question. "And yes, she's a genuine psychic."

"So, you know her?" Dennis asked.

He and Tamara had not yet joined the team when Isabelle Adams worked as a consultant. They only became part of the BAU during the last year.

"Yes. Galen, Fiona, and I have worked with her before."

"What's she like?" Tamara asked.

"See for yourself." Galen nodded toward the door.

Everyone turned as Gib opened the door and held it for Dr. Adams.

"Whoa," Dennis whispered under his breath.

Leo silently echoed that sentiment. It was or had been, Izzi's style to dress in a hippie fashion, natural fabrics, flowing skirts with peasant tops, and belts made of woven hemp rope or knotted cotton. Her jewelry was typically of silver and gemstones, and her shoes were never leather.

Her style made her stand out, but in a manner that gave the impression she was the grandchild of some of the original Woodstock hippies who'd cross-bred with the Fae. Today, the fairy hippie child was gone. In its place was a woman who would literally stop traffic.

Izzi stopped and looked around the room, then removed the hooded blood-red cloak, revealing her outfit, one that came as a surprise to Leo.

The waist-length cascade of white hair had been cut in layers, still long but framing her face in a manner similar to the pixie style she'd worn when he first met her. Her eyebrows and eyelashes were still dark and thick, and her skin as creamy as when she was seventeen.

Today her clothing said one thing. Power.

From the blood-red of the cloak, the all-black beneath it formed a sharp contrast. A form-fitting black turtleneck top and black skirt clung to her figure to just below the hips and then flared out into an irregular fluttering hem, covering her to mid-shin. Black and what he suspected were fake leather low heeled boots peeked out from beneath the skirt.

A big opal in a silver frame hung from a thick chain around her neck, and silver bracelets with gemstones like amber and amethyst, jade and moonstone, decorated her wrists.

There's been a time when her aura was that of a young fairy, a creature of magic abilities who'd suffered from the evil in this world yet survived with an appearance that made her look like a princess to be protected and loved. Today she was every inch a woman who'd realized her power. The princess was gone. In her place was a queen.

She stood still for a few moments, and her eyes moved over the people gathered in the room. The first person she acknowledged was Fiona.

"Fiona." She hurried across the room. When Fiona stood, Izzi hugged her. "It's so good to see you again. You look wonderful. Thank you for the beautiful holiday card."

"You're welcome, and thank you for that amazing homemade jam and the incense." Fiona smiled when the embrace ended. "And damn girl, you look amazing."

"Still as kind as ever." Izzi returned the smile. "Thank you."

Then she turned her attention to Galen and extended her hand. "Galen, hello. You never change. Still breaking hearts and cracking cases, I'm assuming."

"Always." He took her hand, and she covered their clasped hands with her free one.

"It's good to see you, Galen."

"And you, Isabelle."

She smiled and turned her attention to Leo. For a moment, time stood still. At least for him. She surprised him by stepping close and hugging him. "Leo Sebastian," she said softly. "I've missed you."

"And I've missed you." He returned the embrace, then smiled at her when she stepped back.

"I hope we can find a moment to catch up?" The way she had to tilt her head back to look up at him reminded him of her petite stature.

"We will," he promised, then looked at Tamara and Dennis. "Let me introduce you to the rest of the team."

Leo watched as Izzi shook hands and told Dennis and Tamara what an honor it was to meet them. She'd charmed both of them in under a minute. She then looked across the room at Gib. "Special Agent in Charge Foster has offered me a position as a civilian consultant, and I first want to say what an honor it is to work with all of you. I hope I can prove myself to be an asset.

"Second," she looked around at everyone, "when can we get started?"

"My kind of woman," Dennis said, then looked a bit aghast, like he'd overstepped some boundary.

Izzi just laughed. "I can see we're going to get along just fine. So, I've read the case files on the Cheerleader and the latest on the Seven Bridges murders. Where are we going first, and what else do I need to know?"

"Sit." Fiona indicated a vacant chair beside her.

Izzi sat, and within minutes, everyone was seated at the table, and all attention was on the cases.

Leo marveled that Izzi handled it all so well. The last time he saw her, she was, for lack of a better word, broken. Now she seemed strong, confident, and ready to do battle.

He looked over at her and caught her eye, and she gave him a wink, then gave her attention back to Tamara, who was speaking. Leo noticed Gib watching Izzi, and wondered what had transpired, how he'd convinced her to come back and work with them.

Two hours passed before Gib, who had stepped out to take a phone call, returned, and asked for silence. Leo had noticed him leave and wondered what it was about. It looked like they were about to find out.

"There are new developments in Mississippi on the Seven Bridges case," Gib announced.

"A hair found at the scene and a shoe print match that of a man found in a car at the bottom of a ravine last night. Why the car went off the road has not yet been determined, but the victim had more than his own blood on his clothing, and his shoe matched a print found at the last scene in New Allenton."

"Are we still leaving this evening?" Fiona asked.

"No. Wheels up in two hours. Get what you need."

Everyone started gathering up their things, folders, laptops, tablets, and phones. Leo stayed seated, as did Izzi. Once everyone but he, she, and Gib left, he spoke directly to Izzi. "Are you sure about doing this?"

"I am."

"Yes, I suppose you are, or you wouldn't be here. But, are you here because of Gib or because that fire

I thought the Seven Bridges Unsub extinguished has flamed back to life, and you want to get back to the job of catching him?"

Izzi looked directly at him. "Both. But I don't think we will catch him in Mississippi."

"Why?" He couldn't put a pin in it, but something about that statement made him distinctly uncomfortable. Did she know something she wasn't sharing? Leo hated mistrusting Izzi, but it'd been a while and the last time he was her she was pretty messed up, so he needed to feel confident she was capable of handling this.

She gave him a look that made him feel she'd just read his thoughts. "You know why, Leo. Because he wouldn't leave clues. Not a hair, certainly not a footprint, and I don't believe it's him in that car."

"Or you don't want to believe." He knew his tone was challenging and had meant it to be.

"Do you?" She seemed unaffected by his tone.

"I don't know. If it's not, then why does evidence link the deceased to the crime?"

"Either it's a copycat or the Unsub set it up."

"Do you think he's that good?"

"I do."

"Okay, so back to my question. You're here because…"

"Because Gib asked me. Because I miss working with all of you. Because this is my case more than it's anyone's. Because I realized I don't want to be alone. Because I can help and I'm good at what I do. Because I need to put an end to this guy and because I love Gib and need him in my life. Is all or any of that a problem?"

For the first time since she'd shown up, Leo's apprehension faded. "Not for me. You know that. But I needed to understand what your end game is here."

"To help this unit, however I can, and to put an end to my monster."

Leo nodded. "That's all I needed to know."

"Is it? Don't you want to know if I'm doing this for justice or revenge?"

"Do you know which it is?"

"I do. It's neither. I'm not qualified to determine what merits as justice for what this monster has done, and I don't believe in revenge. But I do believe it's right to stand up again, and if possible, put an end to evil

162

and those who would do evil against the innocent."

"Not just capture, convict, and imprison, but to end. You said that twice."

"Yes, I did."

"So, you are telling me that your need for – what, retribution– sanctions the taking of a life?

"Not at all. I'm saying the need to keep this monster from killing more people validates the need to end him. He is beyond redemption, without remorse, and no one in this country should have one single dime of their tax dollars spent to keep him alive. Not even for a day."

It hurt Leo to hear the sincerity in her voice. She wasn't putting on an act. She was hunting to kill. It saddened him, made him feel that something beautiful and pure had been lost, something that couldn't be replaced.

"What happened to your light, Izzi?"

"What do you think is guiding me, Leo?"

"Light? The light calls for blood?"

"You're putting words in my mouth. I didn't say that. I said, *end* him. And the only way to end that kind of darkness is to drag it kicking and screaming into the light, where its evil is revealed. Not just to us, but to him. And that will end him. The darkness will be destroyed, and that corrupted soul will be taken by the light, and no more evil can come from it."

Leo felt the hair stand up on his skin at her words, and at the way her eyes went white. He looked at Gib, and for a moment, they just stared at one another. Finally, Gib shook his head and ran his hand down the sides of his mustache and chin.

"Do you know how to drag him into the light?" Leo asked.

"Not yet, but in time I will. Anything else?"

"No. Not at the moment."

"Okay then." She stood. "Are we ready to go see who this man in the car at the bottom of the ravine is?"

"Are you sure it's not our Unsub?" Gib asked.

"Absolutely," she replied and headed for the door.

Gib looked at Leo, who shrugged and followed her. After a moment, Gib did as well.

Chapter Nine

Tupelo, Mississippi

Izzi opened the door of her room and held it for Gib to enter. As silly as it would seem to others, she didn't like being the first person to enter a hotel room. Having Gib cross the threshold first helped to dispel the energy from previous occupants. She knew he wasn't convinced that energy existed, but she was, and lucky for her, he didn't complain or try to make her feel embarrassed about it.

Gib checked everything, the closet, bathroom, and the door to the balcony. They'd already deposited his luggage in his room, which adjoined hers, and he'd unlocked the interconnecting door from his side. Now, he unlocked the door from her side and opened it.

"Thank you." She walked in, pulling her luggage.

"You don't have to thank me. Do you want to change or get something to eat before we leave to view the scene?"

"Actually, yes. I'd like to change into slacks. Can you stay and talk to me while I do?"

There was a moment's hesitation that caused her to pause. "If it makes you uncomfortable–"

She didn't stop to think that the year since they'd been together had changed things enough that her changing in front of him would be an issue.

"I wouldn't use that word exactly," he answered and then smiled. "But seeing you take off your clothes definitely has an effect."

Izzi smiled in relief, and as he took a seat in the chair beside the bed, she hoisted her pull-along onto the bed and teased, "Careful, SAC Foster. You could get a girl worked up with all that flattery."

"No flattery, just fact."

This time when she looked at him their gazes held, and she felt heat suffuse her skin. To cover her sudden self-consciousness, she opened her bag and took out a pair of black jeans. Izzy sat to take off her boots, then stood and slid the skirt down, aware Gib was watching and that she had only a pair of pantyhose and lace underwear on beneath the skirt.

"Do you ever wonder if the original profile of my monster is wrong?" she asked as she peeled off the

166

pantyhose.

"What makes you ask?"

"Just a thought." She slid the jeans up her legs and fastened them. "I know this Unsub has been discussed at length time and again, but on the way here, I was thinking. I was seven when he came to our house, and I remember a grown man. At least his size was, and the sound of his voice. It wasn't a young man or an old man, but a man, maybe like my dad, but then again older, or maybe younger."

"And?"

Izzi fished a pair of socks from her luggage and sat to put them on. "So, let's say, for the sake of argument, he was – what, forty, when he came to my house. That was twenty-five years ago. He'd be sixty-five years old now."

"We've considered that. Many times, as you well know."

"But never thought to reassess?" She picked up her skirt, shook it, and then walked over to the closet to take out a hanger for it.

"Why would we?"

"Because I wasn't abducted by an old man in 2018. Because the person who is committing the crimes now, the one who's been killing people for at least the last eight years, is not an old man. Think about his victims. Some were women of size. And strength. He wouldn't have had such an easy time overpowering them."

Izzi returned to the bed, closed the suitcase, and took a seat, facing Gib.

"He would if he's big enough," he argued.

Izzi nodded and crossed her legs Indian fashion. "I remember my mother getting shoved into the room where Donny and I were playing. I could see him behind her, or at least his head in that scary black thing that covered his whole head. I could see down to his lips over her head."

Gib leaned forward, propping his arms on his knees. "And your mother was what, five-five?"

"Five-six according to the coroner's report."

"Okay, so if she was five-six, and you could see from his lips to the top of his head, he'd have to have been around six feet?"

"Give or take an inch. And he wasn't huge, not big like you, or even tall and thin like Leo. He was more like Dennis or Galen. Average size, not big, not fat, just normal."

Gib nodded. "I see your point. If the Unsub is in his sixties, and even if he is still in reasonably good health, he'd have a tough time manhandling some of his victims. Like this last one. She was five-ten, a hundred and forty-nine pounds, and in good shape. She coached girls' basketball at the middle school, and was a regular at the local gym."

"Exactly. So how did he overpower her so easily? From the looks of her body, she put up a fight. There are a lot of defensive wounds, so many it makes you wonder if he didn't walk away pretty beat up. Wouldn't that gain notice? From someone?"

"All good questions, and we'll put them to the team," he said and stood. "But for now, we need to get moving. Anything you need to do before we leave? Want to go down to the café and grab some food to eat on the way?"

Izzi shook her head. "The last thing I want is a full belly to go visit a crime scene."

"Good point. Okay, I'm group texting the team. Want to head downstairs?"

"Sure."

She grabbed her shoulder bag that contained her wallet and personal belongings, phone, and iPad, and then grabbed a short wool jacket from her luggage.

Gib finished texting and opened the door for her. Izzi stopped at the door and looked up at him. "Can I confess something to you?"

"Anything."

"I'm a little scared."

"Of?"

"Being at the scene."

"It's not the first time you've visited a crime scene."

"No, but it's the first time I've visited one of his since … you know."

"Since you were kidnapped and held captive and I was stabbed and nearly died."

Izzi nodded. Gib took her hand and gave it a squeeze. "If you find yourself getting overwhelmed, just walk outside. Text me if you need reinforcement."

"Thank you."

"What are friends for?"

His smile helped to ease her as much as his touch.

Crime scene –New Allenton

The county sheriff had two deputies waiting for them, along with an investigator from the MBI, the Mississippi Bureau of Investigations. Everyone piled out of the van as soon as Galen, who'd volunteered to drive, stopped at the end of the gravel driveway.

Izzi sat there for a few moments, looking at the house. Leo looked back and saw her, then retraced his steps. "Are you okay?"

"Yes, fine."

"Then why are you sitting here?"

"Just waiting."

"For?"

"There's a lot of people gathered in front, getting ready to go in. A lot of energy and emotions, expectations, and questions. It's too much to filter through. At least for me. I thought I'd wait. Once everyone goes in, maybe I'll walk around outside and see if anything strikes me."

"Want some company?"

"Do you want to keep me company?"

"Absolutely."

"Then yes, thank you."

When Leo smiled at her, Izzi felt that connection between them, the bond of friendship, and a shared past. "While we have a moment, I wanted to say thank you," she said.

"For what?"

"Kindness, friendship, passion – teaching me that sex without love is empty, and sex with love is a thing of beauty. Showing me that caring continues even when passion ends and for nearly dying to try and keep me out of harm's way. I'm sorry if anything I did hurt you or your family, Leo. That was never my intention."

She saw the glisten in his eyes and reached for his hand. He smiled and blinked several times. "You always have had a way of getting to me. And I told you a long time ago that you never have to thank me or say you're sorry. You risked just as much for me, and if anyone is responsible for hurting my family, it's me."

"But you're okay now, right? You and Margaux? And Ayanna?"

"Yes, we are. And by the way, thank you for

befriending them. They're always so delighted to hear from you, to get a card, and those care packages you send are always a hit."

"I like them. They're good people, and Ayanna is really something, Leo. The best of you and Margaux just shines in her. You should be proud."

"We are. But enough of that. Tell me about you. How are you? Really?"

"Making it," she answered honestly. "And better since Gib showed up. Ironically, the thing I was running from was the thing I needed the most and now I realize that. I'm ready to find this monster, Leo. And this time, beat him."

Just then, Gib motioned for Leo. "Sorry," Leo apologized. "You ready to join?"

"Not just yet, but you go on. He obviously needs you."

He smiled and hurried toward Gib. Izzi saw him pass Galen, Tamara, and Dennis, who were standing together with the MBI officer. Galen spoke, and Leo stopped. A moment later, everyone looked in her direction, then Leo continued to where Gib waited.

Izzi was surprised when Galen walked away from the group and over to where she sat in the van. "Are you hesitant to go inside?"

"Hesitant?" She looked at the house and then at him.

"It's as good a word as any. You don't have to, you know."

"But I need to."

"Why?"

"To feel it was really him."

"You think that's possible?"

"I know it is."

"But you don't want to."

"I do, but – well, maybe I'm just chicken."

"I don't think that's a description anyone would ascribe to you, Isabelle."

Surprise number two.

"Well, thank you. So, what do you think?"

"I think I'm ready find out if you're up for this."

"To catch a killer? Are you?"

"I'm always ready for that. You think we can?"

"Not today."

"Why?"

She considered it for a moment. Galen had not always been supportive of her insights, and he made no effort to hide the fact that he didn't put much stock in psychic intuition, but he also had always listened and considered what she had to say, even if he turned around and discounted it.

But this was a new time, and she was no longer inexperienced and hesitant. Besides, it was long past time for her to trust herself and him. "I can't tell you. I just know that nothing's clear today, and I think that's how he wants it."

"Care to elaborate?"

"Yes, but let's walk," she said as she watched everyone file into the house.

Izzi led the way down the drive and into the rutted gravel road that ran in front of the house. "Did you notice there are no houses in sight of one another?"

Galen frowned, looked one way, the other, and then back at her. "You're right. I honestly hadn't paid attention."

"And no one who's been interviewed could remember seeing a car in the driveway or parked on the side of the road."

"That doesn't mean there wasn't one."

"Or that there was," she said as she turned and started back the way they'd driven to reach the house. Something was pulling her in that direction, some intangible thread of energy.

She could hear Galen's footfall a half a step behind her and feel his curiosity, but it didn't interfere. The energy stopped pulling but didn't disappear. Izzy looked around, unsure what direction to look or what to look for.

She blinked as it hit her. "Look," she pointed, "across the road. Is that a path?"

Together they crossed the road. Sure enough, a beaten path led away from the road and down the hill, disappearing into the trees. Just two feet off the path was a footprint. They looked at it and then at one another.

"Are you thinking what I'm thinking?" Galen asked.

"That maybe he didn't drive in?" She turned and started back in the direction of the house.

"And that if we follow this path, maybe we find out whether the dead guy in the car is a copycat killer or our Unsub played a new game with us."

"I'm betting on the latter."

"Why is that?"

"Because he likes to constantly remind us that he's smarter."

"And does this make him smarter?"

"That depends."

"On?"

"On whether we find something he didn't mean for us to find or if he's covered his tracks so completely that we're just a pack of puppies chasing our tails while he sits back and smiles."

"I don't particularly like the puppy imagery."

Izzi chuckled. "No, I don't imagine you do. But then you're a little like him, aren't you?"

"Me? How?"

"You like being the smartest one in the room."

"Doesn't everyone?"

"Good point."

She stopped when she reached the gravel sidewalk that led to the front door. "Are you ready?" He asked as he looked from her to the house.

"As I'll get. Let's do this."

"After you."

She nodded, pulled on a pair of gloves, and took a step. Izzi felt it when she crossed the threshold. It was like pushing through a membrane. There was resistance, and then suddenly, she was surrounded, enveloped in the pain and fear that'd seeped into the walls and floors and ceiling. It permeated everything in the house and got stronger with each step she took.

By the time she reached the bedroom, she could barely breathe.

"Iz?"

Gib took her hand and tried to steer her away from the doorway. "Are you okay? Maybe you should–"

She knew he was trying to help and loved him for it, but it wasn't what she needed. His concern added to her anxiety rather than diminishing it. He didn't think she could handle it. She wasn't strong enough. This was a mistake.

Doubts can be contagious. She couldn't let his doubts become hers. So, she drew on her reserves and pulled away from him. "I'm fine, Gib."

"Iz–"

"Fine. Seriously. Just let me do this my way, okay?"

"Yes." He nodded. "Of course. If you need me..."

"Thank you." She gave his arm a brief squeeze, then stepped into the bedroom.

Oh god. It took every ounce of her will to take another step. *No, please. Please, oh, God, please. Don't hurt my children.*

Izzy put her hand to her lips, to keep any sound from emerging. She could hear the cries of the children: the wail of an infant and the terror of two older children. Not old enough to understand but old enough to know the horror they were trapped in.

She felt in the pocket of her jeans for her worry stone and formed a fist around it as soon as it was in her hand. Even through the glove, she could feel the stone grow hot. The air in the room seemed alive as if it possessed substance. It was like a bowl of water that shook, rippled, and waved when touched or impacted by an outside source.

Images appeared and vanished, too quickly to recognize, and in such rapid succession, they made no sense. Izzi didn't try to make sense of any of it. She now understood what she was experiencing. The residual energy of what had happened. It was stored here.

Show me. She stopped trying to make sense of it and stepped into the energy. That's when everything went quiet and still. Izzi wandered the room slowly, stopping after one step to look, smell, and listen. The crime became clearer, a movie that played in her head, horrible and inhuman.

Her heart beat faster.

Sweat beaded on her forehead, ran down the middle of her back. She was so close. So close to touching his essence, to knowing him. As if reaching for something physical, she extended her hand and touched the door of the closet where empty handcuffs hung from a hook screwed into the surface. They were encased in a plastic bag that had been taped closed.

She didn't need to touch them. Just the door. One more step and she was close enough to place the palms of both hands on the door.

Pain the likes of which she'd never imagined, seized her, stabbing into her chest with enough force to rob her of breath. She couldn't get her lungs to work, couldn't inhale. Couldn't see. Oh god, she was blind.

Panic had her fingers clawing at the surface of the door as she gasped for air. Izzi couldn't scream for help, couldn't separate herself from the poor woman who'd died here. *Help.*

As if in answer to her plea, someone pulled her away from the door and turned her around. Immediately her vision returned, and she could once again breathe. Izzi blinked and looked up into Galen's eyes.

And the world went silent. Calm.

"You're okay," he said softly. "Do you hear me? You're okay."

She nodded. She was okay. Strange how quickly that had happened. "Thank you."

"Sure." Galen moved his hands from her shoulders and stepped back a pace. "Can I ask what just happened?"

"I felt her. Terrible pain. She couldn't breathe."

"He had her against this door," Galen revealed.

"Yes. He stabbed her twice in the left lung and once in the right. She was bleeding out when he took her heart."

"Correct."

"And he left no prints, not one hair or skin cell. Not a drop of blood or saliva?"

"Correct."

"And no heart?"

"It hasn't been found. But if this is a copycat killing, it may not be found. The killer might have kept it."

"And died with it in a car accident? I don't think so." Izzi looked around. Now that she'd been taken by the energy, made to feel the pain and had moved beyond it, she could pay attention to other things. She took her time, looking around the room, stopping to close her eyes and absorb what energy the objects possessed. There was nothing more for her here. She walked back over to where Galen stood with Dennis.

"Can we talk?"

"Sure."

She led him out into the hallway. "Would you consider going to Gib and asking if we can have someone follow that path and see where it leads?"

"I would consider it if you tell me why."

"Because I think he's playing with us, and I need to know what's at the end of that path."

"Fine, but it's getting dark soon, so we'll request they do it at first light."

"Thank you."

"Don't. I'm going to be straight with him and say the request comes from you but that I support it. That way, if it's a wild goose chase, it's your bird we're chasing and not mine."

Izzi shrugged. "Fair enough."

He headed for the front of the house, and she made her way into the kitchen and out onto the back stoop. Not so long ago, a woman and her three children called this place home. Now all they'd known and loved was gone. Their future was wiped away because a monster found them, one who delighted in the agony of others.

Now, this was a place permeated with horror and death, and until the monster paid for his sins, it would never be clean. *Please let us find him.* She sent out a silent wish.

Sadly, she was not shocked to hear a whisper in reply.

Not today, my love.

Not until you're ready to be mine.

Izzi's eyes moved, her gaze searching the darkness. Was he out there? Watching? She couldn't tell. She didn't think he'd be reckless enough to come so close.

That gave her a thought. Something she'd discuss with the others when the time came. Perhaps what they should be doing was challenging him to come closer. Make the game personal. If he won, he got her. And if he lost, she got him.

And then he would cease to be.

Chapter Ten

"First one up, as usual."

Gib looked behind him to see Galen standing at the coffee station. "Hotel beds," he said in the way of an explanation.

The truth was, he wasn't sure he wanted to tell anyone what had really kept him awake. When the team returned to the hotel the previous evening, they were given the use of a conference room. Once they'd eaten, they went over the evidence that had previously been collected at the crime scene, looked at all the photos again, and discussed their observations.

Izzi listened to everyone without volunteering to add or argue. He found it odd that she didn't contribute in any way. When the discussion wound down, he finally looked at her. "Is there anything you want to add?"

"I'd prefer to wait until we visit the scene of the crash and speak with the ME if that's all right."

"Absolutely."

"Great. Well, I'm pooped, so goodnight everyone. Rest well."

She practically ran from the room. Everyone else left but Leo and Galen. Gib looked at Leo. "What did I miss?"

"Beats me." He cut a look at Galen. "She stuck with you most of the time, so maybe you have some insight?"

"I'm not sure. All I can tell you is that when she went into the bedroom, something happened. She went to the closet door, where the Unsub killed the woman, put her hands flat on it, and every bit of color drained out of her face. She was gasping for breath and looked like she was about to fall.

"I went to her and turned her around, and her eyes were white. It was creepy. It was like she was in a fugue state or something. Then she blinked. I told her she was okay, just to breathe, and she did. She said she felt the victim's pain."

He looked at Gib. "I wasn't aware she had such an ability. She said the woman was stabbed twice in the left lung, once in the right, and was bleeding out when he took her heart."

"That matches the ME's report," Leo offered.

"I'm aware, and I don't mind telling you that took me by surprise."

"I know what you mean," Leo agreed and looked at Gib. "Maybe you should check on her?"

"Maybe so." Gib stood. "Thank you. See you in the morning."

"Get some rest," Leo said and was echoed by Galen. "Sleep well."

Gib went to his room and found the interconnecting door between his and Izzie's room open. There were no lights on, and he wondered if she was already in bed. He tapped on the doorframe and waited for a response.

"Come in." She turned from where she stood in front of the sliding glass doors to the balcony.

"Are you okay, Iz?"

"No."

Her directness shocked him. Izzi typically avoided admitting to any kind of weakness. "What can I do?"

She hurried to him and threw herself into his arms. "He was there, Gib. At the crime scene."

That delivered a jolt. "What do you mean he was there?"

"I heard him. In my head. I was standing in the kitchen, thinking how sad it was. Once a family lived there, a woman with hopes and dreams for her children, doing what she could to make a good life for them.

"I bet there was a time they were all in that kitchen while she made cookies, times when she fixed pancakes or a birthday cake, or they had hotdogs. Times they laughed and smiled, and love filled that little house.

"Then he showed up, and he turned it into a tomb – a place of horror and death. He took everything from them and then just walked away. I wished that we could find him. End him. And then I heard him. In my head."

"What did he say?"

"Not today, my love. Not until you're ready to be mine."

Gib held her tighter. "That's never going to happen, Iz. I'll kill him with my own hands before I let him touch you again. I swear on my life."

"I know and I love you for it. I do have a request,

and it's going to seem strange."

"Ask anyway."

"I'd like to work more with Galen."

"Can I ask why?"

"Because he doesn't care about me. God, that came out wrong. What I meant is we're not close. With you and Leo I'm always picking up on your worry for me, and, not to be insulting or make you mad, but it can be distracting. I love you for it, but it makes it hard to do what I do. With Galen it's different. There's nothing coming from him to interfere with my insights or my own thoughts."

"I wouldn't be insulted by that, and yes, in the field, stick with him if you need to partner up. I'll mention it to Leo so that it appears to come from me."

"Thank you."

"You don't have to thank me. Is there anything else I can do?"

She didn't reply for such a long time he thought perhaps he'd said the wrong thing. Then he heard her whisper, "Promise me we'll close this case, Gib. I want us to find and stop him so we can finally have a life. A real one. One with a home and a dog and two cats and maybe a bird."

Gib smiled.

"That sounds damn good to me, Iz. I thought that maybe once we stop this Unsub, it might be time for me to try my luck in the private sector."

"Seriously?" She pulled back and looked up at him.

"Seriously."

Her smile was genuine and filled him with relief, and with hope. He hadn't lied. She'd have known if he did. Ever since she'd agreed to work with him, he'd been thinking about it. And he thought about it as soon as he woke this morning.

Now, he tried to put it out of his mind as Galen took a seat at the table with him.

"You look like a man who didn't sleep," Galen commented.

"And you look the same whether you sleep or not. Listen, before everyone else gets here, while we're at the crime scene, could you stick close to Iz? She has a harder time getting impressions when Leo or I are close. She picks up on our concern for her, and it's a distraction."

"Sure," Galen agreed. "It makes sense."

"I appreciate it."

"Don't mention it." Galen looked over Gib's shoulder. "Looks like the troops are amassing. I'm going to grab some food from the breakfast buffet while there's time."

"Of course."

Within minutes everyone except Izzi was seated at the table, eating and discussing the day's schedule. Initially, they planned to visit the site of the car crash where the man's body was found that the police believed to be the Unsub. Gib had revised the plan after speaking with Izzi and Galen. Now, he, Galen, Izzi, and Fiona were going back to the home where the family was killed. They would be accompanied by a forensic team from the state who would take impressions of the footprints Izzi and Galen found and see where the footprints led. The rest of the unit would go to the crash site and wait for Gib and his group there.

Gib saw Izzi arrive as everyone else was finishing their breakfast. He rose, and just as he started toward her, Fiona stepped up beside her at the coffee station. "Do you want to grab something to eat on the way?" Fiona asked.

"No, this is about all I can handle in the morning," Izzi smiled, capped her cup, and looked around Fiona at Gib. "Good morning."

"Good morning."

"So, what's the plan?"

"You, Fiona, and Galen are going with me to get a look at those footprints you and Galen found. A forensic team from the state will meet us there to take impressions. We'll rendezvous with the others at the scene of the car crash."

"Sounds like a plan."

"Do you have everything you need?"

"I do."

"I'll get Galen."

"Great."

She looked at Fiona. "Let's walk outside. Looks like a pretty morning."

It was nice, with a clear sky and air that held more than a bit of cold. Still, with a cloudless sky, it wouldn't be bad to be outside. Izzi drew in a deep breath, then looked at Fiona, who was watching her. "What?"

"Just wondering."

"Wondering what?"

"If you're still the same. I know it's only been a year, but things change – people change."

"Do they?"

Izzi didn't know that she agreed with that statement. "Really? How many people have you known who've actually changed?"

Fiona frowned and was silent for a few moments, then replied, "Good question. I mean, I know people who've made changes – stopped drinking or smoking, things like that. That's change."

"That's giving up a pattern of behavior. Not change. I'm betting they're still the same people. Nothing has changed about who they are, just *what* they do. And how many of them just found another addiction? Health, food, exercise, sex, dancing, cooking, you name it."

"Good point, and I guess people don't change, but honestly, you don't seem the same to me. When you left, you seemed ..."

"Go ahead, you can say it, Fi."

"Okay then, you seemed broken somehow. Small and fragile and –and broken."

"Probably because I was."

"Because of being that psycho's captive?"

"No. Because of Gib almost dying."

"But he made it, Izzi, and you could have stayed."

"No, I couldn't. I wanted to, but I wasn't strong enough."

"For what?"

"For fear that it would happen again, and when it did, I'd lose someone I cared about. For good. I couldn't take that chance."

"Especially with him?" Fiona inclined her head toward the building.

Izzi looked at Fiona and smiled. "Yes."

"I get it. Everyone does. I mean, the ones of us who've been with the team for a while and worked with you and Gib."

"Really?" Izzi had often wondered what the people on the team thought of her and Gib as a couple.

"Yeah, really. You brought him back to life. Even his kids say that."

"They're just being kind."

"No, they're not and you know it. Neither am I. You did bring him back, and when you left, it broke him too."

"That wasn't my intention."

"I believe you, but you need to think long and strong about why you're here, Izzi, because every day that you are, Gib will lose more control over those restraints he put in place, holding his emotions in."

"What are you trying to tell me?"

"That I don't want you to break him again."

"I won't."

"Are you sure about that? I mean, how is it different now?"

Izzi considered her answer before speaking. She and Fiona were friends, but she wasn't in the habit of confiding in people or sharing certain parts of her life. Still, she knew Fiona and all the unit cared deeply about Gib, so she gave the short but truthful answer.

"I realized that while I *can* live without him, I don't want to. Not even for a day."

"Because you're still in love with him."

"Yes."

"Good enough for me. Him too, I imagine. Here they come."

Within a couple of minutes, they were in the car and on their way. Izzi opted to sit in the backseat. Fiona climbed in beside her, leaving Galen the front passenger seat. Gib drove, and once they were on the road leading to the crime scene, he initiated a conversation. "Galen, I want to hear from you and Izzi again on these footprints and their significance."

Galen turned his body to cut a look back over his shoulder at Izzi. "You want to take this?"

"No, thanks, go ahead." It wasn't that she was hesitant to speak, she was simply curious how Galen would frame their request for this part of the investigation.

"Fine." He directed his attention to Gib. "One. It's clear the Unsub didn't drive to the house. It'd rained earlier in the day, a real downpour according to local law enforcement and neighbors who were interviewed. If a car had driven in or out of the driveway, there would have been tire tracks, and there were none.

"Two. If he didn't drive, then he walked, but it stands to reason that he wouldn't walk miles on end.

196

Logically, he'd had found a place to park his car where it wouldn't be spotted, and wasn't far from the victim's home.

"Three. We found footprints, and when I asked one of the deputies, he said that the path was mostly used by kids as a shortcut from Miller's Crossing at the foot of the hill to the victim's road. When asked, he said it wasn't uncommon to find cars parked there. High school kids often parked off-road in the remains of an old driveway to a pasture that was once part of a large local farm. Now, it's just a place for kids to gather to go swim in the small lake there.

"Which means it wouldn't seem out of place to see a parked car, and if the Unsub was continuing his methodical preparations as we assume, he would take care to not appear out of place."

His answer prompted questions from Fiona and Gib. Izzi kept silent, listening and paying attention to the energy in the vehicle.

Every living thing puts off energy, and one of her so-called extra senses was the ability to pick up and interpret that energy. She was quite adept at picking up on it, but interpretation wasn't easy. People were complex, and what might feel like the energy of anxiety might also be excitement. No two people's energy was the same, and their reactions were colored with different genetic and environmental

197

factors. Each brought a unique set of life experiences to bear, which altered their energy to be different from all others.

Still, she could glean a few things. Neither Gib nor Fiona were dismissing the possibility. They leaned in the same general direction as Galen and Izzi. None of them were convinced the Unsub had left such apparent clues. It didn't fit his profile at all.

"Unless he's done," Fiona said.

All talk ceased.

Gib shared a look with Galen, then glanced up into the rearview mirror at Izzi. She looked at Fiona. "What would lead you to that conclusion?"

"The elephant that's been in the room for years that no one wants to acknowledge."

Izzi felt a sudden shift in the energy. Fiona's comment had either upset or shocked both men. Why? "What elephant is that?"

"The age of the Unsub. You were seven when he invaded your home. Your mother was twenty-seven. All the women he picks range from twenty-five to thirty-two. There's never been a victim older or younger, signifying this seven-year span to be meaningful for him."

Since she and Gib had just discussed the age of the Unsub, Izzi found it an odd coincidence that Fiona was now bringing it up, but didn't reveal that. She just nodded. "I agree. And the elephant?"

"His age. How old would you guess him to be? I know you wouldn't have any idea from the first encounter, but you were his prisoner for three months, so you must have some idea of how old he is."

Izzi felt the anticipation of the people in the car. She'd been asked about the Unsub before – anything she could tell that would help identify him. So far, her answers had not proven helpful.

"As I've said before, I never touched him. He took great care not to let that happen. He took great care to make sure our skin never came into contact when I was his captive. If he touched me, he wore protection.

"I never saw his face, looked into his eyes, or heard the true sound of his voice. His mask had some kind of – voice distortion. I don't know what, but it gave his voice a mechanical sound. And he always wore black, covering his head, body, and arms.

"I can say that when he knelt in front of my cage to unlock it or just to talk to me, he didn't seem to have problems kneeling or standing up again. That could indicate a man younger than his late sixties, or a man who'd enjoyed good health and stayed fit."

"Which leaves us where we've been all along," Fiona complained.

A thought seized Izzi. One she'd had more and more over the last year. Since she was seven, she'd been interrogated, interviewed with and without hypnosis, and even undergone regression hypnosis. There were things about that night she could not recall, no matter what technique was employed.

Why had her mind blocked out portions of her memory? Was it of her own volition, or did the Unsub have something to do with it? Was there a way to unlock those memories? She made a mental note to search for answers.

Lost in thought, she let the conversation flow over and around her. When they reached the road where the crime scene was located, she noticed two sheriff's cars parked alongside the road. A van pulled in behind them as they parked, bearing the logo of the state crime lab division.

After introductions were made, Izzi and Galen showed everyone where they found the first footprint. Markers were put into place beside every track discovered, and those assembled followed the path, watching carefully for more. Due to their slow pace and search for any other potential evidence, it took an hour to reach Miller's Crossing. Sure enough, across the road was a piece of land that had seen a lot of car traffic.

There was little to no grass, and thanks to rain and tires, there were sizeable depressions and holes.

Everyone crossed the road and started looking around. Izzi wandered deeper off the road into the trees. There was a path, well-worn on each side with a hump in the middle, obviously formed by tire tracks.

She had a sudden flash.

Teenagers laughing, talking. An old jeep with a cooler of beer. Beach towels. She felt a smile tugging the corners of her mouth.. A lot of young people had followed this path. It must be the way to the lake. She could almost imagine the scene. A hot afternoon, kids swimming and sitting on towels, talking, and laughing.

It seemed idyllic.

Until suddenly, the temperature seemed to drop. She immediately hunched in, crossing her arms tightly.

That's when she heard it.

Humming.

It was the sound of someone happy. In anticipation. Eager.

She whirled around, searching, her eyes moving over the landscape.

It took you long enough. It's a shame you're not smart enough to know what to look for.

Where are you? She kept looking.

Close enough. But not as close as I will be.

"Iz?"

She jerked her head in the direction of Gib's voice. "Are you okay, Iz?"

"I heard him again."

"Here? When?"

"Just now."

"Is he nearby? Do you think he's watching?"

"I don't know."

"What does your instinct tell you?"

"That we need to visit the morgue and talk with the ME about the body they have."

"The locals think that's the Unsub."

"Why?"

"Because of the shoe print. A hair found at the crime scene. Matches the dead guy."

"And what do you think?"

"I don't know. I need to see the evidence. You ready to go? The locals will stay and keep searching, make molds of the prints and compare to the one from the house."

"Okay."

He gestured for her to precede him and then fell in half a step behind her. Iz cut one more look over her shoulder. *Close but not as close as I will be.*

Somehow those words filled her with a horrible certainty that her monster was changing the game on them. That maybe he was tired of his kills and needed more.

Maybe he wanted a more challenging prey to hunt now.

Them.

Chapter Eleven

Izzi could feel the frustration of the people as they headed for their cars. The time they spent with the medical examiner netted information that, in Izzi's opinion, refuted all claims that the deceased could be the Seven Bridges Killer.

Everyone on the BAU team backed her up, but to no avail. The governor instructed the state investigators to close the case. They couldn't afford to have a serial killer running around, being written and talked about in the media. Particularly in an election year.

So, whether the BAU agreed or not, at this point and despite Gib's protests, the local and state police had decided to call a press conference the following morning, announcing they'd solved the murder of the woman, Bonnie Cole, and her children, and that the infamous Seven Bridges Killer was dead. He died when his car went off an embankment as he was fleeing the scene.

Gib was so angry he was stone cold silent. Izzi

knew, as well as anyone under his command, what that meant. When Gib was that quiet, you didn't want to be the one to break his silence. It was scary, and he didn't have to hit you to inflict deep wounds.

Which meant no one was eager to ride back to the hotel with Gib. They had two cars, so the rest of the unit could ride in one, leaving Izzi to ride with Gib. Leo mumbled that she was probably the only person Gib wouldn't eviscerate. She wasn't sure she had immunity from his anger, but didn't argue. In fact, she suggested that the others find a place to eat.

"We're supposed to debrief in conference room B," Tamara argued.

"I'll ask him to have dinner with me and tell him I suggested you all go out. Just a little time for everyone to decompress and get a grip on our frustration so we can take a look with clear heads and see if we can come up with something that will change the governor's mind."

"Just the fact that there was no knife or body part found negates their claim that this is the Seven Bridges Killer," Fiona said. "He always leaves the knife and something from the victim."

"And we've made that clear and it's in our report. It's all we can do," Izzi insisted gently. "For now. Let's just take a beat and give Gib one as well. What if we meet at ten for coffee and dessert? I'll ask the hotel to set it up in the conference room."

"Sounds good," Galen was the first to agree. "And I think Isabelle's right. Let's give Gib some space."

"Fine," Leo consented. "See you later."

"Yes. Enjoy your meal." Izzi hurried over to where Gib stood at the other car waiting.

Leo watched them leave and tossed the keys to Galen. "You drive."

Galen caught the keys, unlocked the car, and got in behind the wheel. "What about that steakhouse just off the highway?"

"Works for me," Dennis said immediately.

"I'm game," Fiona added and looked at Tamara, who was squeezed between her and Dennis.

"Okay by me."

"Then the steakhouse it is." Galen started the car and pulled out.

For the first minute, everyone was quiet, then Leo spoke up. "This is unacceptable." His voice rose with each word.

"I agree," Fiona chimed in. "I know I was hesitant to commit at first, but I don't buy that this guy is the Seven Bridges Killer."

"Nor do I," Galen added. "It doesn't add up."

"No, it doesn't," Dennis offered. "There's always a murder weapon, some kind of blade, found on a bridge. Why not this time?"

"Exactly." Galen cut a quick look at Dennis. "This guy doesn't leave evidence except what he wants us to find and never fails to leave a blade that nets us no clues or leads. There's no reason for him to change his pattern now."

"Which leads us right back to where we were," Leo groused. "Being ridden roughshod by a governor who is more concerned with reelection than catching a criminal."

Galen blew out a breath. "Look, we're just going in circles, so how about we table it for an hour, have a beer, a meal, and try to find something – anything to talk about aside from the Seven Bridges Killer."

"Like the Cheerleader Killer?" Dennis asked. "Has anyone come up with any new ideas on that? We'll be meeting the state police tomorrow, and we need to have some idea what we're going to say."

That turned the conversation. Leo gave a silent thanks to Dennis. Right now, his head was about to explode, and he needed to get clear and calm so he could try and come up with a logical reason to present in defense of keeping the Seven Bridges case open.

What bothered him more than the frustration of believing his team to be right and the locals to be wrong was something he wouldn't voice aloud. What if there was an off chance that he and the others he worked with were wrong and the Seven Bridges Killer was, in fact, dead? Didn't he want to close out that case, that long chapter of his life?

Or did he want to keep the case open *because* it had been such a big part of his life?

Did he not know how to let go of this case and if so, why?

*****

Izzi didn't say a word; she just stared out of the side window as Gib drove. When his phone rang, he pulled off onto the shoulder of the road, turned on his blinkers, and answered.

"SAC Foster."

He looked at Izzi as he listened. She estimated that it took about forty seconds. "Thank you. Yes, I appreciate your call."

Gib slid his phone into the breast pocket of his jacket. "In a stroke of luck, or extreme coincidence, local police report some teenagers showed up at the police station last night. They say they were out drinking and partying and on the way home saw something unusual. A fishing pole tied to the rail of a bridge.

"They stopped and untied it and found a knife tied to the line. It was covered in blood. The police turned it over to the state crime lab who just called them to report that the pole has prints that match the dead guy in the car, and the blood matches that of the woman who was murdered.

"The police say it's a done deal. The Seven Bridges Killer is dead."

"That *is* an amazing coincidence. Quite timely," Izzi commented.

"And?"

"And a lie."

"How do you know?"

"Because I felt him. At the crime scene, on the path that led down to Miller's Crossing and when we came out of the morgue. I felt him. He's watching."

"God damn it, Iz!" He whipped around in the seat to full face her. "Why didn't you tell me?" Gib's voice was thunderous in the confines of the car.

With his jaw clenched and his brows lowered, he looked every bit like a man who was eager to hit something, or someone. Hard and repeatedly.

"Yelling isn't going to serve any purpose," she said as calmly as possible. "I've been wanting to talk to you about it, but couldn't until we were alone."

"And now we are. So?"

"So, I have no doubt at all that our Unsub is alive and well. The guy in the car was part of his game. Something new. Something to put us off balance, make us doubt ourselves and put us at odds with local and state law enforcement."

"He wants to embarrass us? Is that what you're saying. He wants to make us look ineffectual? Inept at our jobs?"

"To remind us that he's smarter," she said. "I believe he staged the entire thing."

"That would take an extraordinary amount of forethought, planning, and orchestration. Pulling it off would be nothing close to miraculous. Do you really think he could do it?"

"I do."

"Then walk me through it."

It'd been on her mind all day, and she'd played out a scenario in her head, one that she believed their Unsub could have concocted and carried out. "What if he made friends with the dead guy in the car?

"Set up a time to get together, drink and shoot the shit. Only, he kills the guy, drives his car to where people park all the time at Miller's Crossing, then takes the guys clothes and shoes and wears them. He walks to the victim's home, kills her and her children and then returns to the car, redresses the dead guy and drives the car to the embankment. He then puts the dead guy behind the wheel, pushes it off the embankment and tada–the Seven Bridges Killer for the police to find.

"And what about the fact that the guy in the car is twenty-six years old and couldn't have committed the crimes in '95 because he wasn't born until '94, and during the 2008 to 2010 spree he would have been fourteen to sixteen years old?

"Add to that he was less than six feet tall and small framed. There's no way he overpowered the victim."

"Then how can he expect us to believe he's the killer?" Gib asked. "Does he think we're that

211

stupid?"

"No. I don't think he expects *us* to believe it," she answered.

"Then what's the point?"

"To make the police here believe it. This state has two senators up for reelection, along with their governor and at least one house seat. It's a volatile political climate and their party is scrambling to hold onto power.

"If the Seven Bridges Killer is becoming active again and has chosen Mississippi as his hunting ground, it could hurt them politically.

"Closing the case makes them look good and they'll use it – a lot– in their campaigns. So, it's not about what's true or what does or doesn't make sense. It's about closing this case and making them all look good."

"I get that – believe me. But that doesn't answer the question. What's in it for him?"

That was the question she'd dreaded him asking and knew he would. She didn't want to give voice to her suspicion, but the strength with which it was growing told her she had to. "To make it harder for us. He's changing the games. If the case is closed, we don't have any reason to keep looking for him. At least until he gives us one. As much as I know you don't want to hear this, he's proven one thing with this stunt."

"What?"

"That all we can be is reactionary. We can't be proactive, we can't do or say anything that will stop him from killing again, and even when he does, if it's in our own back yard, we're still two steps behind."

"Then how do we catch him, Iz?"

"We give him a dose of his own medicine."

"Meaning?"

"We don't argue with closing the file. We tell the media the Seven Bridges Killer turned out to be not nearly as smart as he thought. I mean, who doesn't get their car serviced? To die from faulty brakes isn't the mark of brilliance."

Gib looked at her for a moment, then a smile rose on his face. "That will piss him off. We'll be telling the world he's not smart."

Izzi nodded. "And once he's pissed…"

"Oh, hell, Iz. He could go on a killing spree. We can't risk putting innocent people at risk."

"I don't think we will."

"Then what do you think he'll do?"

"I think he'll make us his marks."

"You think he'll go after the BAU agents?"

"I do."

Gib ran his hand over his mustache and down to his chin. "I don't know about this. I'll have to give it some thought. I can't use my people as bait."

"Then come up with another solution. It was just a suggestion."

He nodded. "And a damn good one if it didn't put my people in harm's way."

She smiled. One of the things she loved about Gib was his genuine concern for the safety of his people. She wished she could tell him that the decision might be out of his hands no matter how he felt.

Because she was beginning to feel that their monster was ready to step up from the minors and play with the big boys. And how better to win than to hunt the monster hunters themselves?

And end them all.

One by one, until there was no one left.

But him and her.

Chapter Twelve

Omni Atlanta at CNN Center
Atlanta Georgia

Izzy turned at the sound of the tap on the interconnecting door to Gib's room. "Come in."

"Are you decent?" he asked as he entered.

"Would it matter?" She looked up from the act of taking off her shoes. He'd removed his jacket, tie, shoulder holster, and badge, signaling he needed to step back from being special agent in charge for a little while.

"Actually, not decent might provide a much-needed diversion." He sat on the bed, kicked off his shoes, and leaned back against the stack of pillows at the head of the bed.

She knew what he meant. They'd been in Atlanta for

two days, and the entire team was exhausted. They'd interviewed every cheerleader, team player, coach, trainer, driver, security personnel, and stadium employee, and had viewed every second of security video footage, along with all the footage shot at the game by the various networks.

Gib, as special agent in charge, took it personally that they'd not yet come up with a profile for the spree killer. The old saying "shit rolls downhill" didn't hold true here. It ran uphill. Straight to him. Sure, the agents would be reprimanded, possibly fired if they screwed up bad enough. But Gib caught hell for what all his people did or didn't do and knew their performance was seen as a reflection of his ability to lead a team and get the job done.

Izzi had known Gib for some years and had lived with him long enough to be able to tell when he needed what he called diversion. She called it stress relief. He needed to get out of that part of his head so he could calm down and see things clearer.

It might not be wise, but at the moment, the need to take care of him superseded wisdom. So, she acted on impulse, stood, unzipped her skirt, and slid it down over her hips. She then peeled off the pantyhose and tossed them aside. "Oh god, that feels good. My skin can finally breathe." Izzi ran her fingertips over the skin of her thighs and up to her hips.

She cut a look at Gib to find him smiling. Izzi turned back around, pulled her top up over her head and let it fall, revealing there was nothing else beneath it.

"Tease," Gib said.

"You said you needed a diversion." She turned one shoulder slightly, just enough to look back at him as she slid her panties down and stepped out of them.

"Well, you succeeded. I'm very–diverted."

"Not as much as you will be," she said and hoping she wasn't going to get shot down, turned toward him.

If a look could deliver a touch, his delivered in spades. Sensual, hungry. It was almost tangible, an energy that brushed her skin and inspired need and passion. He let his gaze travel over her, taking his time. When the journey brought him back to her face, his expression made her breath catch.

"Iz."

Dear God. How could he make that syllable sound like the most sacred and vital element of his existence? It undid her. Completely. Her body was in motion before her mind caught up.

Three steps and she reached the bed. A heartbeat later, she was atop him, working at the buckle of his belt. Between the two of them, he was divested of his clothes in less than a minute. Then he pulled her down on top of him.

The low sound he made when their skin made contact reverberated through her. She felt his sensations, the excitement, and need, and projected back her own, mirroring his passion with hers.

All it took was one kiss. Just one. Then her need exploded and took control. She raised up on her knees to reach between them and guide him inside her. In two seconds, Gib took control and rolled her over beneath him.

And then there was no room for thoughts of anything other than their union.

It had been so long, the desire was too intense and her fuse too short. Try as she might to hold back, she succumbed to the hunger. When she cried his name and climaxed, he followed her over the edge.

For a few moments, there was only the sound of their breath, the feel of his heart beating against her chest. Before his weight could settle on her, Gib rolled over onto his back, and she followed, putting her head on his shoulder with one arm and one leg thrown over his body.

Izzi closed her eyes, savoring the moment. She had

no doubt that before morning, she'd be back in his arms. In his bed, or he in hers. They'd kicked open the door she swore to keep locked, and she didn't want to shut it again. No, she wouldn't let that happen.

No matter that Gib had loved another before her, had shared a life with a woman he adored, had a family and still mourned the loss of his wife and the mother of his children. It didn't matter. It wasn't a contest. Izzi loved him. He was her first love, and she knew with certainty, he would be her only.

She didn't want to waste any more time running from what she felt and what she wanted. If it meant she had to help him hunt monsters, then so be it.

"Penny for your thoughts." His voice had her opening her eyes.

"I was wondering. When we get back to Quantico – to your house, maybe I could change my mind about staying in the guest room? Or not. I don't want you to think I'm trying to push–"

"Yes," he interrupted.

"Yes?"

"It's all I've wanted. All I want. So yes, please."

"It's what I want too, so thank you," she agreed, and

then because there was no choice, she turned their attention to what was ahead. "And now, even though I hate changing the subject– Are you going to lead the briefing?"

They were scheduled to brief local law enforcement in under two hours. The next home game started in three and a half hours, and based on the BAU recommendation, law enforcement and stadium security would have some ideas on what to look for.

"Yes."

"Will the press be involved?"

"Possibly. After the briefing, the chief of police is likely to call a press conference."

"And the reason for that?"

"To ease the city, to let people know they're safe."

"Are they?"

"I'm going to go out on a limb and say yes. For the moment, there's no reason to believe this spree is directed at anyone other than cheerleaders."

"Such an odd target, don't you think?" Izzi sat and pulled her knees up to her chest, wrapping her arms around her legs. "I mean, why would someone have it in for these girls? Nothing adds up. No jealous boyfriends or husbands, none of the victims so far have had relationships with swat or military snipers."

She pushed her hair back from her face. "There's nothing to suggest that it's the work of some guy whose girlfriend or wife didn't make the cut. In short, there's no reason. No motive."

"I know." Gib ran both hands over his face. "Nothing about it makes sense. But we better come up with something, or I'm going to end up standing in front of a news crew with my dick in my hand."

"Well, then we'll just have to come up with something." An idea occurred to her. "Oh, wait. Damn, how could I have overlooked it? Remember Galen saying there had to be people other than law enforcement or military who can shoot one of those rifles?"

"Yeah, so?"

"So, what if the killer is someone who's a hunter or a marksman of some sort? Maybe an Olympic shooter. And what if the shooter is a woman?"

"A woman? There's never been a female sniper, spree, or serial killer that I'm aware of."

"Doesn't mean there couldn't be one. Maybe we should have all the women checked out who auditioned for the cheering squads."

"That's definitely an avenue we should explore."

"Now?"

"Actually, I think we still have a little time before we have to meet everyone and go over the strategy we've worked out for tonight's game."

"Do you think having a police presence, even an FBI presence, will make a difference?"

Izzi was the only dissenter against the plan Gib and leaders of local and state law enforcement had agreed upon. She advocated for either calling off the game, not having the cheerleaders present, or having them taken out of the arena from an exit other than their normal avenue.

But in this show, the locals were in charge, and they were dead set on staking out the place. From the location of the last shooting, they believed they now knew all the buildings to target that had line of sight to the exit and parking lot they'd chosen for the women to use.

"I have no clue, and that's what bothers me. All we can do is be vigilant and hope we don't end this evening with another name added to the death toll."

"We'll do whatever you tell us. You know that,

right?"

"I do. But I don't want to think about it anymore right now."

"No?" She trailed the fingers of one hand over his chest and then lower. ""Want to take a shower? I don't know about you, but I'm a bit hesitant to go to work smelling like sex."

"A shower sounds good. Shower sex sounds better."

Izzi giggled when he pulled her to him and rolled off the bed with her in his arms. She didn't believe for one moment that either of them could just wipe all thoughts of the evening ahead from their minds. But if they could find solace and something to cling to other than dread of more death, even for a little while, she was all in.

As it turned out, she did find solace and a lot more. It'd been a long time since she felt surrounded by love and in Gib's arms, and his presence, that's exactly how she felt. For that, she'd give thanks and hope she could return to those feelings at the end of the night.

And not to mourn the loss of another innocent life.

Chapter Thirteen

State Farm Arena, Atlanta, Georgia

Izzi was grateful beyond words that the owner of the team had allowed them to use his private box. The noise in the arena was deafening. She'd never attended a professional basketball game, and within minutes it was clear that fans of both teams were completely absorbed by the game.

Her anxiety had been growing since the moment they arrived. Something in Izzi's gut said this was a terrible plan. But Gib had agreed, which meant she and the rest of the team needed to follow orders and hope things didn't go south.

Because she was better equipped than Tamara or Fiona, she was assigned to rendezvous with the cheerleaders at the end of the game and leave with them. Perhaps she could pick up energy if someone was watching. She wasn't sure she could stretch her senses to encompass such a large area, but she would try. Izzi was convinced there would be another shooting. An hour and a half before game time, maintenance reported a power outage in the garage where the players, cheerleaders, and many season ticket holders parked.

Gib and the local leaders of law enforcement quickly adjusted their plan. The cheerleaders were asked to move their cars to a nearby, uncovered parking lot and to surrender their keys to security. If power was restored to the deck, their vehicles would be moved again.

Efforts were being made to get the power back on, but so far, the parking deck was still dark. This had happened before, at an away game in Charlotte, NC, where the first basketball cheerleader was killed.

"Why wasn't the power outage ever considered?" Izzi leaned over to speak softly to Galen, who sat beside her.

"That's what I'd like to know. In Charlotte, the situation was much the same as here. Locations offering line of sight are minimal. Closing the garage threw it wide open for the shooter."

"I'd say the same is true here. How does law enforcement even know which structures to target?"

"Whichever of their shooters say they have a line of

sight and a high probability of hitting the target."

"That sounds so horribly impersonal, doesn't it?"

"It does," he agreed, then added, "Listen, I know you were opposed to it, but before you walk out that door, put on the vest and cover it with your jacket."

"I'm not the target." She didn't see a need for a bulletproof vest. The spree killer was targeting cheerleaders.

"He might not know that. You'll be with the rest of the squad. Just do what we ask, okay? Wear the vest and keep your earpiece in."

Izzi realized that he, like everyone on their team, was just trying to look out for her.

"Okay, I will. Where will you be?"

"I'm leaving here momentarily to take a position with one of the local teams on a nearby building where we have a good view of the area. Gib will be in the chopper, and the rest of the team will be assisting the locals in the locations considered to be prime."

"Well, you be careful, too."

"I always am."

"Then don't break that habit. You still owe me a drink."

"I owe you?"

"Yeah, you lost the last round of basketball trivia on the way over. Loser buys drinks."

"Oh, yeah, right. Then I'll pay up once we get past this evening."

"I'll look forward to it." She looked up as he stood. "See you later."

"Yes, you will."

She hoped he was right. It wasn't long before a female police officer arrived to escort her to the cheerleaders' locker room where they'd be changing after the game. Izzi chatted with the officer as they waited and learned all about the woman's parents who had immigrated here as children and the challenges they'd faced.

Now, the officer, Sylvia Menendez, was a decorated member of law enforcement, with three children and a husband who worked with the public defender's office. They donated their time and money to help immigrant families and tutor children.

Izzi admired that kind of compassion and giving and said as much. Before she could say more, the cheerleaders arrived. Talk about a change in energy. It was almost overwhelming. They were on a high from performing, and their enthusiasm was practically chaotic.

Izzi could feel the difference in the women. Some were trying to "catch" one of the players, others were hoping their boyfriends or husbands felt just a little threatened by the attention they received during the games and the number of men who hit on them, and others had career goals in mind. They wanted to be noticed and discovered. Life in front of the camera was their goal.

All Izzi wanted at the moment was to escape all that energy. She found it shocking that none of the women were overly worried about the sniper. Izzi knew they'd all been told what to expect, do, and look for as they left.

Did they not remember, or was it a case of what many people fell victim to? No matter what kind of threat, people often had the "but it won't happen to me" mentality. If only they knew how dangerous that attitude could be. Hopefully, with the number of law enforcement working tonight, none of these women would end up a victim. Izzi sent out a silent prayer for that.

When all the women were dressed in their street clothes, Officer Menendez called for attention and went over the instructions again. Once she'd gotten a verbal confirmation that everyone understood, she led them toward the exit.

Izzi brought up with the rear, walking beside a beautiful redhead. The woman gave her a smile. "Hi. I'm Debi."

"Isabelle." Izzi offered a smile.

"So, you're with the FBI?"

"Only as a consultant."

"For what?"

"Psychology."

It wasn't entirely untrue but wasn't much of a conversation starter, either. If she'd said she was a psychic, a conversation would have ensued.

"Oh. Can I ask something personal?"

"Sure."

"Where did you get those contacts? Those are the coolest I've ever seen. Your eyes are like a pastel abalone shell if you know what I mean."

"I do, and thank you, but these are my real eyes."

"Are you kidding? How lucky is that? With that white hair and dark brows, you're rocking the whole hot Fae thing. All you need are the pointed ears."

"Hot Fae?"

"Yeah, you know, in the stories."

"Oh, yes, of course."

She didn't have a clue, but Debi was broadcasting like a reality show, so it wasn't hard to figure out. Just as she opened her mouth to ask titles of books about hot Fae, Officer Menendez stopped at the exit.

With the way the women were talking and checking their phones, Izzi couldn't help but wonder again why they were not at all concerned by the possible danger they were in.

That changed the moment Officer Menendez opened her mouth to give them instructions. By the time they walked outside, they were clinging to one another, looking around fearfully as Officer Menendez instructed them to proceed to their cars.

The woman Izzi walked with, Debi, took hold of Izzi's arm. "Are you scared?"

"Cautious," Izzi replied, hating that she felt like she was telling a lie. She could justify her answer, keeping the woman calm, trusting law enforcement had a secure net on the area, and would stop the killer if he or she acted.

As she walked, trying to validate her answer, without warning, all the hair on her body felt like it suddenly stood on end. Something like a spider web of electricity danced over her. Danger. Before she could react, a voice sounded in her mind.

His voice.

If you're smart, you'll kiss pavement, my love.

"Get down!" she screamed as she shoved Debi between two cards and dropped to the ground, grabbed Debi by the arm, and pulled her down as well. "Stay down," she ordered. Izzi crept on hands and knees to the rear of the car.

"Can you hear me?" She hoped her comm unit was working.

"Loud and clear. What happened?" Gib's voice came back to her.

"He's here."

"What? He?" There was a moment's pause before he continued. "Iz, are you–"

A distant report from a weapon was followed by screams from the parking lot.. "Oh god." Izzi felt a wave of nausea as she saw a woman on the ground. The front of her head was – missing. Women were screaming and running as Officer Menendez tried to get them to stop.

"Get between the cars!" Izzi shouted. "Between the cars! Get on the ground."

"We have to get out of here!" Debi tried to take Izzi's arm.

"No, we have to do exactly what we're doing. He can't see us here, so this is the safest place until the police arrive. Just stay down, okay?"

Debi didn't look convinced but nodded and crouched lower. Izzi turned her attention to Gib's voice in her earpiece, calling her name. "I'm here, I'm here."

"Tell me."

"There's one woman down. Dead. We're facing – hold on." She took out her phone and activated the compass app. "Okay, we're facing east. From the position of the body and the wound, the shots had to have come from the west or maybe west southwest."

"The federal center," he said, clearly to someone other than her.

As she waited, another voice intruded, this one from inside her mind. *M.L.K and Forsythe, Isabelle. They better hurry. I feel the need to end this particular game.*

What do you mean by this particular game? She waited, but there was no answer.

"Gib!"

She said his name twice before he responded. "Stay put, Izzi, and keep those women on the ground behind the cars."

"M.L.K and Forsythe, Gib. That's where the shooter is. Hurry. And have someone radio Officer Menendez and update her."

"Will do."

In under two minutes, she heard sirens. "Gib?"

"We have a jumper."

"What?"

"A woman. She stepped off the building. Leo and Galen are on the roof. The rifle is there."

"Anything else?"

"What else would there be?"

"Check the shooter. Was she stabbed?"

"What would make you–"

"Tell them to check!"

She heard him giving orders. "I'll get back to you, Iz. Sit tight."

Like there was any other choice. Luckily, the place was swarming with police in minutes. Officers coaxed women to their feet and from behind cars to escort them back inside the stadium where they'd be sequestered in the locker room until they could be questioned.

"Dr. Adams?" A uniformed officer appeared at the end of the car where she and Debi sat. "Officer Gordon, ma'am. Are you ladies okay?"

"Fine, thank you, Officer Gordon." Izzi stood and offered her hand to Debi. "If you could see Debi safely to wherever you're having the squad gather, I'd appreciate it."

"That's why I'm here, ma'am."

"Thank you."

"Thank you." Debi gave Izzi a hug before she left with the officer. Izzi smiled and returned the embrace, feeling the relief and the lingering fear that had Debi trembling. "Don't worry, it's over. You're safe."

Debi nodded, swiped at tears, and left with the officer.

"Anyone listening?" Izzi hoped her comm was active.

"On my way to you now." Galen's voice came back to her. "Look to your left."

She spotted him the moment she turned. "I'm here to escort you to the rooftop where we found the shooter's weapon."

"And the shooter?"

"Dead."

"From the fall or something else?"

"What else could it be? We got there after she jumped."

"Did anyone check?"

"Not that I'm aware; the M.E. is in route."

"I need to see the body first."

"Why?"

"Call it a hunch."

"Fine, let's go."

Izzi fell into step with him, noticing the number of looks he received from the cheerleaders. "You seem to collect a fan club wherever you go," she commented.

"What?"

"Take a look around, Romeo."

He did glance around and then at her. "Not interested."

"There are some beautiful women on the cheering team."

"I suppose."

"And you could have a dozen phone numbers if you wanted."

"But, I don't."

"Why?"

"Wow, nosy much?"

Izzi would have taken offense if he hadn't smiled and added. "Just jerking your chain. I guess I've had my fill of beautiful on the outside, and either empty or narcissistic on the inside."

"That's harsh. Do you really believe beautiful

women are that shallow?"

"I think they can be. I don't believe it's a hard and fast rule that applies to every pretty woman."

"And what if one of the women here was destined to be the great love of your life?"

Galen chuckled. "Now that would be a miracle."

She almost asked why but decided against it and slowed her pace as they drew near the street.

It was roped off, with police and emergency vehicles cluttering the pavement. But it wasn't the vehicles or the swarm of people that had her feeling a sudden sick dread. It was the tarp-covered body on the street.

Izzi stopped five feet from the body. People around her talked, took photos, spoke into their radios, and milled around. She just stood there, feeling energy swirl around her from everyone present. It was a mishmash of emotions, ranging from those who were excited to be part of what was happening to those who wished they were anywhere but there.

Izzi looked at Galen to find him watching her. "Can I see her?"

"Come on." He took her arm and suddenly all that eddying energy, all the noise– it just vanished, and for the space of a breath, there was nothing but calm and silence. It was remarkable. Shocking. And more welcome that she could have expressed

"Thank you." She let him lead her to the body.

When Galen released her, all the noise and chaos returned. But she was centered again, and so it didn't throw her mentally off stride.

"Ready?" he asked.

She nodded, and he knelt to pull back the tarp. Izzi staggered, and he bounded to his feet to support her. Once again, she was enveloped in a cocoon of calm. "Thank you," she murmured and then knelt beside the body.

Were you afraid?

The answer Izzi received was not from the victim. Not that she'd expected one. Nor had she expected the voice that did answer in her mind. The fact that he'd heard her unnerved her to no end.

You already know the answer. Why ask the question?

Izzi wasn't about to acknowledge him. "Cause of death?" she asked Galen, who knelt beside her.

"My guess would be that gaping hole in her chest."

"Not the fall?"

"I'm betting she was dead before she left the roof."

Izzi looked up at the building. "Can we go up there?"

"If you want."

"I do."

"Can I ask why?"

Her first inclination was to make up a plausible excuse, but she owed him honesty. "I want to see if I can pick up a particular energy."

"What particular energy?"

That wasn't a question she was ready to answer. "Ask me after I've gotten a look around."

"Fine."

Keeping secrets, my love?

Izzi felt her fingers curling into her palms until her hands were white-knuckled fists. She wouldn't give him the satisfaction of acknowledging his presence. The last thing she wanted him to realize was how it terrified her to think he was somehow involved in what had happened here today.

She needed her wits about her to ignore him so she could have a clear head. Her gaze swept over the scene, searching for Gib. As a rule, she was stronger when he was near, but she knew how worried he'd been about her returning to work with the team, and she didn't sense his usual well of calm.

That thought had her suddenly looking at Galen. Aside from Gib, she'd never felt swathed in stillness. Not until today. Until Galen touched her. To say it was remarkable was putting it mildly. It was a complete shock, particularly since she and Galen had never been close.

Why would he provide such a deep well of calm and sense of safety? Did it have something to do with her not being able to read him aside from superficial thoughts? She was curious and growing more so each time it happened.

She lost herself thinking about it, and he remained silent until they arrived at the door that opened onto the roof. She reached for the door handle, but he took her arm and stopped her. "Are you sure you want to do this? I don't understand what it is you really do or hear or feel, but I've seen the effect it has on you, and I have to ask. Are you sure about this?"

"I am. I need to. But I also need a favor."

"What?"

"Stay close? Sometimes touch helps shield me from things that are too difficult."

"You got it." He reached around her and opened the door.

The moment they walked out onto the roof, she was hit with it. Turmoil, confusion, hurt, and anger, all jumbled into a chaotic blend. She followed the trail of energy, letting impressions come and go like quick flashes of motion clips of a video playing in her mind, one on top of the other, sound and light mixing and blending with such force that her brain struggled to simply take it in.

And then she came to the edge of the building where a sniper's rifle lay with an evidence marker beside it. There was also a cartridge. One. She'd fired once. Izzi looked out from the building, and suddenly she was taken by a vision.

Everything was ready.

She was ready. As ready as she could be. She thought this time would be easier. It wasn't. Why was she doing this? Was this the price of love? Of passion?

What kind of love was that?

She turned away from the sight of the city beneath

her. She'd pack up and leave. He'd never know. She'd find a way to excuse herself. Keep him. Keep him? That was funny. She'd never had him. He had her.

Her eyes closed as memories of his touch wrapped around her, making her weak with longing. If she didn't do this, she'd lose him.

"You're not going to disappoint me, are you, love?"

Eyes that were closed popped open wide. She'd not expected him to be here. That both excited and terrified her.

"Show me your talent, darling," he said from behind her, put his hands on her shoulders, and turned her, steering her back to her weapon.

She had no strength to argue, no will to refuse what he wanted. With skill born of practice, she took her place, looked through the eyepiece, and waited for the moment. She didn't have to wait long. She zeroed in on a blonde woman and smoothly pulled the trigger.

"Brilliant," he said from behind her as she watched blood and brains blow from the opposite side of the woman's head from the bullet's entry.

She turned to face him with a smile on her face,

eager for his praise. When the pain hit, digging deep into her body just below her diaphragm and then shooting up, she couldn't even gasp.

Izzi yanked herself back from the vision, surprised by the revelation, horrified to realize he hadn't lied. This was his game. "Oh god." She looked at Galen. "Where's Gib. I need Gib."

"On my way." She heard his voice in her earpiece.

"Tell me what's happening," Galen said. "Isabelle, talk to me."

"Can't. Not yet." She wasn't lying. She had to let the rest of the impressions she'd receive rise to the surface. She needed to make sense of it, search it. If he'd been here, if the woman saw him, then maybe she could get a glimpse of his face.

Not yet, my love.

Not until we finish the game.

Her control slipped, and the thought was out before she could stop it. *What game? What do you want?*

Why, to end them, dear one. All of them.

Everyone you care for, everyone you've lusted for or loved. I'm going to end them all. And then, well, then you'll be mine.

His voice made her twitch, and she reactively reached out for the closest human contact.

Galen. She took his hand, and he turned to look at her. "It's okay," he assured her.

"No, it's not," she blurted. "Not at all."

"Because?"

"He's here, Galen. He's here. He's the one who killed her."

"He who?"

"The Seven Bridges Killer."

"Isabelle, that's —"

"Don't say crazy. This is his kill. His game."

"Game?"

She almost didn't say it, but she wouldn't leave Galen hanging with that anxious expression on his face and the sense of dread she felt coming faintly from him. "He's changed the game. This is all his doing. I'm betting we'll find something to prove she was doing this for someone. A man. He used her as his weapon."

"But why?"

"To prove we can't stop him. Can't beat him."

"You're saying he sees this as a game?"

"I am."

"And what are the rules?"

"I don't know, but I'm guessing it's survival."

"Whose?"

She paused for a beat, then answered. "Ours."

Chapter Fourteen

Atlanta, Georgia

"Okay, spill." Galen slid into the driver's seat of the car and turned to look at Izzi, who sat in the back seat.

Izzi watched Gib, who stood beside the car with the police chief. "On?" She turned her attention to Galen.

"That comment you made on this game being about our survival."

"Oh, I will, but can we wait until Gib and Leo are in the car?"

"Sure."

Neither one of them spoke again. Leo walked over to where Gib and the police chief were standing, and after another minute or so, the chief shook hands with him and Gib, turned, and left. Leo got into the front passenger seat, leaving Gib the seat beside Izzi in the back.

Gib reached over to squeeze her hand as soon as he was in the car. "You okay?"

"Yes, thank you."

"Why did that yes not sound like a yes?"

Izzi noticed Galen turn his head and saw his reflection in the rearview mirror, looking at her. "Something is off about this shooting." She looked at Gib as she answered.

"Such as?"

"Several things." She angled toward him as much as the seat belt would allow. He seemed to sense her discomfort and took her hand, this time hanging onto it.

Gratitude made her feel a little weak. She wished she could share what she felt with him, let him know how his touch comforted her, how his strength gave her courage. She'd love to share all that with him, but if she could, would he then also see her terror?

The idea that her monster was hunting them filled her with a sick dread. Not as much for herself as for him and the others. She knew the barbarism her monster was capable of and had no doubt he'd top his own acts of brutality.

She was scared for the people she loved and didn't know how to stop the monster from his quest. From what he called his game.

As if sensing her fear, Gib spoke gently. "If you're not ready, this can wait."

Izzi didn't think she'd ever be ready but knew the longer she waited, the harder it would be to speak the words. It was the equivalent of yanking out a splinter. Just take a breath and do it.

"No, I need to tell you. When the cheerleaders were being escorted from the stadium, I heard him."

"Him?"

"The Seven Bridges Killer."

"As in for real, or psychically?" Leo asked.

"The latter."

"What did he say?" By now, Leo had turned to look at her.

"Just before the cheerleader was shot, he said, 'If you're smart, you'll kiss pavement, my love,'" and after she was shot, he told me where the shooter was.

"What, exactly, did he say?" Galen asked.

"He said, "MLK and Forsythe, Isabelle. They better hurry. I feel the need to end this particular game."' She nearly blurted out that he'd somehow managed to hear her thoughts when she wondered if the shooter had jumped, but held back that bit of information. She'd tell Gib later, in private. It wasn't something she wanted anyone else to know.

"Why would he do that?" Galen asked. "Give you that information?"

"I told you before. This spree killing isn't what it seems at all."

"Then what is it?" Leo asked.'

"It's a game. His game."

"I'm not following." Leo looked from her to Gib.

Gib immediately echoed Leo's comment. "I need you to be specific, Iz."

She nodded. She'd been trying to stall until all the pieces had clicked in her mind. "Here's what I can tell you with certainty. The woman who died today, the shooter? You won't find evidence that points to a motive. Not in her history or her present life. What you may find, if we're lucky, is something indicating she had a new man in her life.

"A man she was desperate, and I do mean desperate to please. She hadn't ever felt that way about anyone. She was obsessed with him. When he said he had a way she could prove her love, she jumped at the chance."

"Hold on."

Izzi looked at Leo, and he continued, "This is something you picked up from the rooftop?"

"And the body," Izzi answered.

"Continue, please," Gib said and shot Leo a look she read to mean, *be quiet.*

"I picked up a lot of flashes, memories, feelings. After the first murder, he rewarded her. Spent the weekend with her, cooked with her, watched movies she wanted to see, danced in the kitchen while they prepared meals. And they had amazing sex. The best she ever had. He could be gentle or rough, vanilla or kinky. Whatever she wanted, and she wanted it all."

"Can I interrupt?" Galen asked.

Izzi looked at Gib, and while he didn't look pleased, he agreed. "Fine."

251

"Thanks. So, you picked up all this, but it doesn't tell us how she planned or executed her kills. Nor does it tell us why."

"You're right. And she didn't plan it. He did. She just followed the plan he laid out for her, and her success earned her a reward. At least it did, to begin with."

"And today?" he asked.

"Today wasn't for her. She was, after all, just a means to an end. He killed her for his own pleasure. The spectacle of it was for us."

"Meaning?" Gib asked.

"Meaning he wants us to know he's changing the rules of the game. He'll continue to kill or to plan the kills, but from now on, he'll be hunting very specific quarry."

"I suddenly feel like I'm going to hate the answer to this question," Galen said. "But what quarry?"

"Us."

"Us? As in the people in this car?"

"And the rest of the people on the team." Izzi looked at Gib. "He's hunting the people in the BAU. And what makes that more frightening is somehow he's found a way to watch us."

"Oh damn," Leo groaned. "Is this a repeat of 2012?"

Galen cut a look at Leo and then in the rearview mirror at Gib. Gib muttered a curse under his breath. "Son of a bitch."

When he looked at Izzi, she knew what he was thinking. Her own mind was hurtling back in time. To 2012. The year the Seven Bridges Killer almost killed Leo.

2012

In all the time since she first started as a consultant with the BAU in 2008, Izzi had never taken part in a stakeout. She wasn't sure if she was excited or scared. Maybe it was a combination of both. Usually, when she worked with the BAU, it was at Quantico, going over the evidence, visiting crime scenes, and in the case of witnesses or survivors, speaking with them to gain impressions or information.

This was her first time in the field, and she was ridden with anxiety, fearing she would somehow screw up.

She sat in a waiting room on the second floor with a BAU agent, Fiona Metcalf. Both wore comm units, and she could hear the conversation between agents as they took up positions in the hospital.

They were here in hopes of stopping a serial killer suspected to have killed five patients with lethal doses of drugs. After months of exhaustive work, they thought they had uncovered the identity of the killer. A nurse who only worked occasionally, filling in for staff who were on vacation or out sick.

So far, he was on duty during every murder. Gib convinced the hospital to call the nurse, explaining they needed him immediately due to a member of the staff suddenly falling ill. They cooperated, and the suspect was due to report within the next half hour.

Izzi felt the tension. It was almost like the hum of an electrical wire vibrating fast and hard. Time seemed to tick by slowly, leaving her free to let her mind wander.

Since the day Gib first came to meet her, he and the members of the BAU had been part of her life. She often worked one or two cases a year with them, and thanks to that working relationship, she was able to coax them into giving guest lectures at the university where she taught.

She and Leo's short-lived affair had not prevented them from being friends, or her developing a friendship with his wife, Margaux, whom Izzi liked and enjoyed spending time with, along with his daughter, Ayanna.

For someone who'd spent most of her life alone, she found herself thinking of the members of the unit as a kind of long-distance family. Gib's wife, Diana, had certainly made her feel welcome and treated Izzi like one of her own whenever Izzi was at Quantico.

Izzi loved Diana, and thought of her as a friend, but not as a mother figure. That was probably because if she did, she'd then have to think of Gib as a father figure, and what she saw in him was anything but fatherly.

To her shame, she'd had a crush on him since the day they met, and time had not dimmed it. But if there was one thing she was good at, it was hiding her feelings, so as far as he knew, they were friends and nothing more.

"Hey." Galen entered the room, interrupting her thoughts. She realized he was addressing Fiona. "Any chance someone can listen in on our comms?"

"You mean someone in the hospital? Security, maybe?"

"Can you head for security and check it out? This guy isn't showing up, and local PD says he's not at home. Gib wants to make sure he hasn't somehow tapped into our comms."

"I'll grab Ken and head for security. You going to keep Izzi company?"

"Sure," he agreed.

Fiona hurried from the room, and Galen took a seat across from Izzi. "Sense anything?"

"No. Why would you think this substitute nurse would be able to tap into our communications?"

"We're just covering all the bases."

"Well, that's smart. Are you sure he's not in the hospital?"

"No one has seen him, and he hasn't logged in."

"Then maybe he —" All at once pain stabbed her, breath-stealing, body-doubling-over pain. "Leo!"

"Whoa, hold on!" Galen caught her before she toppled out of the chair, and the moment he touched her, the pain vanished. "Are you okay?"

She nodded and pushed him back so she could stand. That's when the pain returned, and she knew for sure she was feeling Leo's pain. "We have to find Leo. Now! He's hurt."

Galen wasted no time putting out the call, then followed Izzi as she ran from the room, pulled by an invisible thread to the stairs, up two flights, and then onto the floor.

"Isabelle, wait!"

She ignored Galen, continuing as fast as her legs would carry her, being pulled by that filament of energy connecting her to Leo. She could feel him and his pain. His heartbeat thundered in her ears, his labored breath constricted her chest. She had to get to him.

Izzi shoved a door open and rushed inside. Leo lay on the floor in a pool of blood. "Get help!" she screamed as she threw herself down beside Leo. Galen skidded to a stop just as she pressed down on Leo's back, trying to staunch the flow of blood.

"Doctors!" she screamed. "Get doctors!"

He turned, shouting as he ran. Izzi turned her attention to Leo. "Stay with me, Leo. Help is coming. Stay with me."

Within seconds medical personnel was moving her aside to take over. Leo was loaded onto a gurney and rushed to surgery. Izzi watched, trying to hold it together as she leaned against a bed for support.

"I told you I'd always be close. Watching.

You should have paid more attention, my love."

That voice. God, she hated that voice. Her monster.

Izzi knew she couldn't respond. If she did, she gave him what he wanted. Attention.

Gib ran into the room, took one look at her, and gathered her in his arms, despite the blood that covered her. His strength allowed her to fall apart, at least for a moment. She clung to him, feeling his vitality warm and comfort her.

"Are you okay, Iz? Were you hurt?"

"No. I'm fine."

"Did you see? Who did this?"

"Him."

"Him? The nurse, Paul Regent?"

"No. Him. The Seven Bridges Killer."

Gib pulled back and stared at her in disbelief. "That's impossible."

Just then, they both heard the voice in their comm units. It was Fiona. "They found Regent in the morgue, on a table. His heart is missing."

Gib and Izzi looked at one another. "How the hell could he have known?" Gib asked.

She shook her head, not yet willing to answer that question. At least not until she knew how to respond. Was she the reason he knew what was going on? Had he tapped into her thoughts?

No. Izzi knew she'd kept her thoughts shielded. She'd spent her life fortifying her barriers.

Then how did he know?

Izzi pulled her thoughts back to the present and looked at Gib. "This time is different."

"How?"

"In the Killer Nurse case, he showed us he could change the rules of the game, use other killers to further his goals. He could not only find other serial killers but somehow learn their plans and use them to show us once again how smart he is. After all, he got a kill out of it, didn't he? And he almost killed Leo.

"Now there's this. It's another step in the evolution of his power. Convincing others to kill for him and then rewarding them by murdering them."

That's when it came to her. As if she'd suddenly taken a dive into his psyche, she saw it.

"Oh god, that's it? Why didn't I see it before? He's

using unpredictability to his advantage. The killer nurse in 2012, the Mississippi misdirection, killing that man and somehow placing his footprint and hair at the scene, and now this case. It all seems to lack consistency. These actions veer far off target from his typical pattern of kills. And it's all to keep us off balance and unable to explain his moves.

"In short, he's using this strategy and the messages he gives me for one reason. To intimidate and terrorize. That diminishes our power and increases his."

Everyone was quiet for a few moments, then Galen said, "I get it. He's thrown down the gauntlet. He wants us to know that it's his game and we don't have a choice. He'll control the playing field, forcing us to defend."

"Exactly," Izzi agreed.

Gib's voice, when he finally spoke, was as deadly serious as she'd ever heard. "I'm going to bury that bastard. If it's the last thing, I do."

"Amen to that," Leo agreed.

"Vigilante justice?" Galen asked.

"You have a problem with that?" Leo asked.

"Nope, I'm in."

Izzi bit her lip to keep from whimpering as the whisper sounded in her mind. *I promise you, mine will be the last face they see. You could prevent it, love. All you have to do is give yourself to me. This time for keeps.*

That confirmed what she already knew. She had to figure out a way to make him think he was getting through to her, to use his need to touch her mind against him.

Because like Gib, she fully intended to destroy her monster.

Chapter Fifteen

Quantico, Virginia

Izzi stopped outside the front door and waited as Gib carried their luggage inside. He paused in the foyer and looked back at her. She didn't move, and finally, he set down the luggage and returned to her. "Is something wrong?"

"Yes."

"Then tell me."

She figured now was as good a time as any to say what she needed him to know. "I'm sorry."

"For what?"

"I was wrong. Back then. I thought I was saving you

by leaving."

Gib was silent for a moment, but she felt the wave of hurt that drifted through him. "I won't lie to you. It hurt. Still does, I guess. But I won't condemn you for the decision. If I thought it would save you, I'd disappear and never been seen again. As much as it'd hurt, I'd do it to save you."

"We're quite a pair, aren't we?" She reached up and tugged gently on his necktie.

"I guess," he agreed. "That makes twice you've left me."

"You know why I left the first time. If I'd stayed … well, you know."

"I do. To be honest, I was grateful. As much as it hurt, it was easier not having you around, reminding me of my guilt."

"Don't say that. We didn't–"

"I know. But I wanted to."

Izzi nodded and put her arms around him. She did know. Now, like so many times, moments rushed back to remind her of her feelings for him.

2012

Izzi sat on the bench beside the ornamental pond, looking out over the water, trying to tap into the serenity of the place. She hadn't slept in days and yesterday she finally came to a decision. It wasn't easy or one that made her happy, but she knew it was the right thing to do.

Now, all she had to do was find the courage to stick with it. That was going to be the most difficult part.

She'd asked Gib to meet her here, away from work and from Quantico. Here no one would recognize either of them. She needed that anonymity and security. What she had to say to him was difficult, and she couldn't do it in a place filled with the energy of people they knew.

"Penny for your thoughts."

She smiled as she looked up at him. "You snuck up on me."

"You must really have been lost in thought."

"I guess so." She patted the bench. "Sit with me."

He took a seat, stretched out his long legs in front of him, and let out a breath. "It's nice here. Tranquil."

"Yes."

"I'm guessing you needed tranquility for whatever it

is you want to tell me?"

"Yes. Tranquility. Courage."

"Courage?"

He changed position, angling with the leg closest to her, crooked on the bench, and his arm stretched out along its back, his hand lightly on her back. "When have you ever needed courage to talk to me?"

"More times than you can imagine."

He seemed genuinely surprised. "I had no idea. I'm sorry. I never meant to make you feel uncertain about the trust between us."

"It's not that." She decided she might as well snatch the tape off the wound.

"Then what?"

"I think you already know." For the first time she looked directly at him.

"Iz, I–"

"Please, just let me say what I need to say."

"Okay."

She took a breath, gathering her thoughts and trying

to clamp down on emotions. "I remember when you came to see me that first time. My first thought was I wished I was older. I wished you weren't married. I know it doesn't make me seem like a very good person, but that was my first reaction.

"I knew you weren't there to recruit me as a friend or lover, but as a tool to help you make the world safer. You were there to offer me a chance to learn, and even though I'd have eagerly accepted more, I was excited to accept you as a mentor.

"Over time, you became more than that. You forgave me for my affair with Leo, and understood that it was the rashness of youth, and a good measure of loneliness that had me becoming involved with a married man.

"I appreciated your honesty and your demand that I break it off. I'll always appreciate that because it was the right thing to do. You became a good friend, one I trusted and admired. Depended on. I felt honored to be accepted by your family and asked to dinner when I was in Quantico. Diana is a lovely, gracious woman and I care deeply for her."

"She cares for you, too."

"I know, and I'll always be grateful for that. And guilty."

"Guilty?"

"Yes. I've asked myself a thousand times, how could I have let it happen? How could I care so much about her as a friend and be in love with her husband?"

She heard the slight intake of his breath, paused, and looked out over the water. "That's why I have to go. I can't stay here, Gib, or I'll screw up. I'll let it grow stronger than my ability to defend against, and —and then you'll either have to rebuke me, or we'll betray your wife, and I don't want to do that. This isn't one of those stories that have a happy ending for everyone. I won't try and break up your marriage, and I can't be around you all the time and not want you, so I have to go."

Izzi allowed herself to sink into memories of that time. When she left Quantico that next day, she felt like her heart was irreparably broken. The following year was misery. She struggled to keep him out of her mind, to focus on her studies. She tried to forget him by getting involved with others.

It didn't work.

Nothing did.

Gib had his own memories to contend with about

their past. He'd not been blind to her feelings for him. It was clear in the energy that arced between them every time their gazes met. He heard it in her voice. It permeated the atmosphere, and if he was honest, he'd admit, he reveled in it, craved and yes, loved her with an intensity he thought had been lost with age.

Shame had been his constant companion those days. Shame for the way he felt about Izzi, a woman so much younger than he, shame that he could feel that way about someone other than his wife.

He still loved Diana and didn't want to lose her. But he couldn't have it both ways and knew if Izzi stayed, he would one day slip and admit his feelings. One day he'd give in to that pressing urge and touch her. Kiss her.

And then he would lose everything.

So, he tried to ignore his feelings, did everything he could to prove himself to be a good husband and father, and when Izzi walked away, he felt an odd sense of relief.

At least his heartbreak was her doing and not his own.

What a coward he'd been.

Gib turned away from thoughts of the past. They couldn't change what had already happened; the past was fixed. The future wasn't. "Are you leaving again?"

She pulled back and looked up at him. "No, but I'm scared it's the wrong decision."

"Why?"

"Because I hear him, Gib. He talks to me and I hear him, as clearly as I hear you now. Once, I thought he just broadcast his thoughts and had no clue if I heard him. I was wrong. He knows I can hear him. I thought I could hide from him, but he's known where I am all along."

"Are you sure about that?"

"I am now."

"Why?"

"Because he knew where I was going." She pointed to the decorative metal bench in the covered entrance of his house. Gib looked, then stepped over and picked up a metal on a ribbon. "A silver Olympic medal?" He looked at her with a confused expression.

"I'm betting if you have it checked out, you'll find it belongs to the woman he killed in Atlanta, the

269

Cheerleader Shooter."

His brows lowered and his face flushed. "Son of a –
" The rest of the sound he made was more a roar than
a word. He hurled the medal against the brick of the
house. "That psycho was at my home?"

"Yes."

"So, he thinks this – stunt, is going to what? Scare
me? Stop me from hunting him?"

"No. He thinks it's going to enrage you, throw you
off balance, and make it easier for him to win the
next round."

"The next round? You make it sound like some
game."

"To him, it is."

"Well, it's not for me." He stomped into the house
and turned, looking at her with a cross expression.
"Are you coming in?"

Her first reaction was to ignore his tone and
expression. If she reacted in kind, it would only fuel
his anger. *Which might be exactly what he needs.*
She realized she was tiptoeing around him, trying to
protect him from what he felt when she should
encourage him to let it out, so it didn't just stay
locked inside, simmering and growing hotter.

So, she changed tactics. She threw her hands on her hips and stuck her chin up. "You want to alter that tone, mister?"

"Isabelle, get inside. I'm not in the mood–"

"Isabelle?" She marched up to him. "Did you just reprimand me?"

"No, I –"

"Oh, I think you did. And I don't think I like it." She walked by him and cut a look over her shoulder. "One little bit."

"And I don't care much for your behavior."

"Well, that's just too bad, special sgent in charge Foster, because you're off duty now and not my boss."

"You're deliberately trying to pick a fight, aren't you?"

Izzi didn't want to smile, but she couldn't help it. "How am I doing?"

"Horrible," he said and made a grab for her.

She squealed and took off through the house. She made it to the family room before he caught her. They laughed, wrestled around, kissed, and touched, and just as he reached for his necktie to loosen it, he looked out of the French doors at the patio and pool area. His expression changed to rage faster than a blink.

She turned her gaze to see what had caused such a reaction. One look sent sick fear washing through her, that suffocating feeling of terror-induced nausea that made your heart race and lungs feel constricted.

A message was scrawled on the glass, broken into interrupted sentences, thanks to the wooden panes. *Welcome home, SAC Foster. Enjoy your lover while you can. The clock is ticking.*

"Son-of-a-"

Izzi interrupted him as he cursed and pulled his phone from his jacket. "Wait." She covered the face of his phone with her hand.

Gib snatched it away from her and pointed toward the door. "Damn it all, you're right. It's him. He's been to my house."

"I know. And you're reacting just like he intended."

She knew her words would hit like a slap, and from his expression, he took it that way. His head jerked and his gaze pinned her. "Would you care to explain?"

"Sure." She softened her tone. "He wants you to be angry, to feel violated and unsafe. This is your home. He's stood on your doorstep, walked around your patio, wrote on your door. He hopes the anger and fear will throw you off balance and you won't be paying attention to what's important."

"Which is?"

"What comes next. He says it's his game and I believe he'll do anything to win because winning proves he's better. Smarter."

Gib put his phone on the coffee table, removed his jacket, and threw it over the back of the couch. He then sat and removed his necktie.

"Then, we need to find a way to return the favor. Throw *him* off balance."

"Exactly." She kicked off her shoes and sat beside him.

"Now, tell me what you're *not* saying." He pinned her with a look that reminded her of his unique talent. The ability to interpret the space *between* the words, what people didn't say.

"We use the communication between him and me against him."

"How exactly?"

"That's something we'll have to figure out. All of us. But the first thing is to turn his stunt back on him. He said for you to enjoy your lover. Then, by all means, do that. He can't pick up anything from me that I willfully block, but he can sense me, so I'll only allow him to sense what I want him to–namely that while he repulses me, you excite me. While I hate him, I love you.

"With luck that will make him mad, and anger will throw him off his game. Then we can come up with a plan that separates one member of the unit from everyone else, making that person his target. He said he was going to take us all out, so let's give him a target."

"And nail him."

"To the wall," she agreed.

"I like the way you think, Dr. Adams." He gave her a smile. "And later on, I plan on showing you how much, but for now, I need to get a forensic team here, just in case there's any evidence that might help lead us to him."

"Then make the call, SAC Foster. I'm not going anywhere but to unpack."

Gib gave her a quick kiss and picked up his phone to make the call.

Izzi retrieved her suitcase and carried it upstairs to the master bedroom. She saw it the moment she entered the room and screamed for Gib. On the bed was a map, a bloody map with a knife stabbed into it. Into the state of Tennessee.

Catch me if you can.

Izzi felt rage rise hot and fast. *Count on it. I'm going to end you.*

She'd reached the end of the line on trying to follow morality and see this killer as a damaged man who needed help. He was a monster. A deliberate monster who, like a rabid animal, needed to be put down.

Fast. Before he hurt anyone else.

behind the
ROCKNG
HORSE

PART 3

The world is a dangerous place to live; not
because of the people who are evil, but because
of the people who don't do anything about it.

-Albert Einstein

Chapter Sixteen

Quantico, Virginia

Izzi had a bit of trouble focusing on what she was doing with agents watching her every move. While she knew they were present because the house was now part of an investigation, being watched made her slightly uncomfortable. Nonetheless, they needed to leave. Neither she or Gib had yet had a chance to unpack what they're returned with today.

She wasn't afraid, just a bit uncomfortable and a little edgy. That wasn't attributable to the agent, but the man who'd violated Gib's home. Izzi added some density to her shields, as she liked to call the mental screen she used to filter out the energy of others. The welcome they'd received upon returning home was something that carried significant weight.

Things had jumped to an entirely new level. With

this move, her monster had announced himself to the entire law enforcement world. He was, without revealing himself, not only claiming credit but delivering a threat– or perhaps in his mind, a reminder and a promise.

He said he was changing the game – that it was his game. And he'd been clear about his goals.

What puzzled Izzi was that after the grandiose moves earlier today, why was her monster silent? That surprised her. She'd expected to be tormented, trying to keep him blocked. But the opposite was true. She couldn't sense him at all. She'd been sending out tendrils of energy for over an hour now, searching. Inviting. And there was no answer to her call.

Something had happened.

The thought appeared as the companion to another feeling, something beneath the conscious layers. He was not in control. Was that what she felt? With her curiousty heightened, she added more energy to her efforts, letting her body go through the familiar motions of preparing to leave.

What she wouldn't be taking with her, Izzi left in the laundry room hamper. Sooner or later, they would return, and she'd do laundry. Until then, it wasn't worth concern.

Gib walked into the room. "Are you about ready?"

"I am. And I packed for you." She gestured to the open suitcase on the bed. "You might want to check."

"I'm sure it will be fine. We should be back here in forty-eight hours, tops."

"Okay." She grabbed the handle of her luggage as he zipped his. "Should I call and book us a room at a nearby hotel?"

"Already taken care of. We'll check in later. Right now, the team is assembling at headquarters, so we need to get over there."

"Fine."

She wasn't surprised the team wanted to huddle, so to speak. Their leader had been threatened, however slight, and they were ready to circle the wagons and come up with a plan of action.

Her thoughts were along those lines, and she could tell Gib was caught up thinking about what happened because neither of them had more than a dozen words to say on the drive to Quantico. The closer they got, the stronger a strange dread grew inside her. By the time Gib parked his car, she felt a bit like a person who already knew the news was bad but was waiting to have it confirmed.

Once inside, in the elevator, she hugged Gib. "When this is all done…"

She could tell he knew what she meant when he hugged her tight, then kissed the top of her head. "Yes, when all this is done, then it's you and me."

"I can't wait." She pulled back and looked at him, seeing his sincerity and his love for her. "You know, it's all I ever really wanted," she admitted.

"Same here." He gave her a quick kiss as the elevator doors opened.

The team was assembled in the conference room. "Talk to me," Gib said the moment they entered. Dennis was on the phone and raised his free hand, with his index finger extended to indicate he was almost finished.

Gib and Izzi headed for the coffee maker. "The forensic team at your house hasn't found anything other than the medal and the message on the glass," Galen said. "Which was written with wax pencil. They'll know more after analysis. The blood on the map appears to be human blood, but again, tests will confirm."

"Any prints?"

"Not a one."

Izzy poured Gib a cup, and just as she handed it to him, Dennis finished his call. "That was the County Sheriff's Department in Tennessee. The map left at your house was no hoax. There was a murder sometime between yesterday afternoon at half-past three when Melinda Jenkins met her children, twins Adam and Alexandra, at the bus stop, and today at noon when Roger Jenkins, the estranged husband, returned from a three-day trip and stopped to drop off presents for the kids.

"It appears to be the work of the Seven Bridges Killer. A twenty-seven-year-old divorcee with two children, a boy, age nine, and a girl, age seven. The boy was found with the mother at the scene. Both dead. The mother's tongue and heart were removed. The girl is missing."

The moment the words of his last sentence had been spoken, Izzi's hand shook so bad she overfilled her cup, spilling hot coffee on her hand. *Oh my God, he has a child.* She turned, putting her back to the room, managed to set the cup on the counter, and grabbed a handful of paper napkins. Only Gib noticed. He tugged on her sleeve, and she whispered "I'm okay." So he turned his attention back to Dennis.

Twenty minutes later, Gib gave the wheel's up order as two hours. The team quickly gathered their belongings and left. They'd discuss the case more on the flight. Gib waited until they were alone, then sat beside her. "What's wrong?"

"The girl."

"The missing girl? What about her?"

"He'll use her against us."

"How do you know? Have you picked up something from him?"

"No. I just ..." she paused before she could say that she knew. That wasn't true. She feared. "What if he tries to use her against us? Or as a bargaining chip? What if–"

"The what-ifs will drive you mad, honey, so stop and let's just focus on trying to find her."

"You know he's nowhere near that scene now."

"He might be. He was watching the Cheerleader Shooter and killed her just minutes before we arrived. He might be tempted to try and observe us again."

"Maybe. But still, what about that little girl, Gib? What if he– what if he's doing to her what he did to me? Or worse?"

"You can't get caught up in that now, Iz. It won't help her or us."

"Then, what will?"

"I don't know, but we'll figure it out. For now, let's wait until we can visit the scene. Perhaps, if what you said is on track, he'll contact you, or will have left something for us that will indicate what his next move might be."

"Okay." Izzi didn't think that was much of a plan at all, but it wasn't time to challenge Gib's authority. Besides, he might have a point. Her monster just might have left a clue for her, something no one but her would notice.

Where are you?

She'd never reached out to him before and wouldn't know, but she did find it more than a bit curious that he'd not responded. He loved to flaunt how connected he was to her, how he could sense her.

Which prompted her to try again. *We're coming for you. Are you ready?*

Izzi was certain that would provoke a response. The fact that it didn't worried her far more than if it had.

*****

He paced the length of the porch and back again, ignoring the growing darkness, aware only of the howls and screams coming from the basement. For a moment, he succumbed and clamped his hands over his ears, trying to mask the sounds. If she didn't stop, it was going to wear him down, erode his control, and then...he didn't want to consider the possibilities. He wanted to keep her. She was perfect– or would be if she would stop that horrible noise.

This is what happens when you unilaterally make a change to the plan. Once it's made, you stick to it. Do you understand?

God he hated being treated like a mental inferior. Yes, he understood. It's not like he hadn't heard this same shit his whole life. *Do it my way. You must do it the way we planned.*

"We planned," he murmured. When had it become this way? Them being separate but together? One always present and listening and one, him, who only heard when his other half wanted him to. When had his opinion not mattered? When had they decided he would just do what the other side of him ordered?

He had just about reached the end of his patience on never being the boss. It was, after all, his handiwork when it came time to torture and kill. His other half didn't have the stomach to do it. Or maybe he was too good to bloody his own hands.

Over the last few years, it had felt more and more like that. His other self wanted the thrill, needed to quench his thirst for their deaths, but wasn't man enough to wield the knife himself. Why was that? Had it always been that way, or had it just taken him this long to see it?

Is that what's important right now?

God, how he hated to answer. He put it off for several minutes until the screams and howls had him clenching his fists, marching back and forth like an animal in a cage. Waiting for the irritation to make him explode into action.

I don't know what's important. What do you want me to do? Kill her? You know that's not why I took her. She's going to be part of our family. She and Isabelle. With them, we'll be complete.

The voice that responded sounded both sad and angry, as if tired of having the same argument over and again. *That wasn't the way we planned to do it.*

He'd forgotten that. Wasn't that strange? It had been the goal for so long. First Isabelle, and then a child they could call their own.

That's what they wanted, him and his other side. He hadn't meant to mess up the plan. He hadn't really planned on taking the girl. Until she challenged him. Called him a coward. Only a coward would tie up a little kid. That's what she said. Even after he blinded her. She still mocked him.

That's when he knew.

She was special. Like Isabelle.

And being special, she would be the perfect child for them. He and Isabelle would love Alexandra and raise her to be like them.

Special and smart.

He could see that future. See Isabelle looking at him with love shining in her eyes. See Isabelle looking at him in passion, stained with the blood of their victim. He'd screw her in the blood. Let it cover them like a sweet balm as he took his fill of her.

You won't do anything with anyone if I can't figure a way out of this mess you've created.

Anger rose, like the first air bubbles as liquid starts to boil. He told himself to hold it together. Do like he'd been taught. Take ten seconds. Just ten. And think about what had brought him to this moment and what his next move should be.

Despite being resentful at being made to feel
inferior, he couldn't fight a lifetime of habit. He
stopped and looked at what had taken place. And
suddenly, he saw how his actions had thrown the
plan out of whack. They were supposed to have
Isabelle, first.

"What do we do?" He stopped pacing.

*You don't do anything but stay put. Gag the child if
you must. I will be with you as soon as possible.
Right now, I have other things to oversee.*

"I could do that, and you could be here-"

*It's your mess, your screw-up. You'll do as I say, and
when I see you, we will figure it out. Until then, stick
to the plan.*

"Yes. Stick to the plan."

Strangely, he was okay with that. This is how things
worked best. How had he forgotten? Don't try to do
all the figuring out of things. He can do that. It's
where he's handy. You stick to what you do best.

Causing pain and death.

Chapter Seventeen

Clarksville, Tennessee

Did you ever see a lassie,
A lassie, a lassie,
Did you ever see a lassie,
Go this way and that?
Go this way and that way,
Go this way and that way,
Did you ever see a lassie,
Go this way and that?

Izzi stumbled and might well have ended up face in the muddy yard if Leo hadn't caught her. "Hey, are you okay?"

"Sorry." She didn't look at him for fear he'd see the lie. Not to mention the fact that it was taking all her self-control to keep from throwing up. "Just caught my toe."

"You're sure?"

"Yes, fine. Go on. I'm right behind you."

"Okay." He released her and continued toward the house. The entire perimeter of the property was cordoned off with crime scene tape. Local law enforcement had officers present to prevent nosey civilians from gaining access. The forensic and investigative teams from the state of Tennessee were busy going over and documenting the crime scene inch-by-inch.

Izzi reached for the hood of the car and steadied herself. She wanted to run and hide, find somewhere safe and huddle up against what had just happened. This was a whole new kind of attack, one she could never have prepared herself.

Nausea bubbled, threatening to rise, and her skin felt uncomfortably moist and hot. Izzi quickly tossed her shoulder bag onto the roof of the SUV and removed her coat. Cold air made her shiver but was a welcome respite as it helped to dissipate the nausea.

"You look like you just saw a ghost."

Izzi looked to her left to see Galen walking around the front of the vehicle. "What gave me away? The white eyes?"

"Very cute, but you're not fooling me. I saw you. You were fine and then suddenly your head jerked up like someone had called your name and that's when you stumbled. Only you didn't look around like most people. You just looked – on alert. So, what's up?"

"Having never been the object of your observation – or at least privy to your impressions, I have to say I'm impressed." That was no lie. He had pretty much described what happened when she heard her monster sing. Even now it gave rise to more goosebumps.

"Isabelle, you don't look well." Galen didn't ask permission to take her arm. He placed his left hand on her back, took hold of her right arm with his free hand, and turned her back in the direction of the SUV's doors.

Izzi felt a wave of something far more potent than cold air appear around her. Soothing and quiet, it was like stepping into a protective bubble. The relief was so great, she literally sagged against him.

"It's okay, I've got you." He supported her, opened the door, and guided her into the seat.

That feeling of protection vanished the moment he no longer had physical contact with her. Izzi almost reached for him, but at that moment, it happened again. The song. And as he sang the words, she was catapulted back in time. To *that* night.

1995

Isabelle retched until there was nothing left in her stomach, and then she dry heaved over and again.

His laughter in her ear made the nightmare more terrifying. If she could only close her eyes, stop having to see it. Poor Donny. His screams had turned to sounds like a wounded animal, whimpers and moans.

She almost opened her mouth to beg, but something inside wouldn't allow it. Some part of herself she didn't even know existed rose up and refused to make another sound, even though she was so scared she was sure her heart would explode.

> Did you ever see a lassie,
> A lassie, a lassie,
> Did you ever see a lassie,
> Go this way and that?
> Go this way and that way,
> Go this way and that way,
> Did you ever see a lassie,
> Go this way and that?

All the while he held her, singing into her ear, the Other laughed and danced. He held her mother around the waist with her back to him, which gave Isabelle full view of her mother's ravaged face and body.

He moved so that her mother's head flopped from side-to-side, and her arms flapped about. It was kind of how Isabelle played with her stuffed animals when she made them move in her make-believe world.

Only now, her mom was in the make-believe of the man in black.

But it wasn't make-believe. It was real.

Izzi wanted more than anything for it not to be. "Please make it go away." She bit her lip the moment the words escaped.

"You don't want to see it?" her tormenter's voice whispered.

"No."

"Well, I think we can take care of that. Can't we?"

The man in black cast her mother aside. Isabelle couldn't stop the tears, but she bit down hard on the lip to keep from making a sound. That's when the man in black stooped down and picked up her mother's heart from the floor where he'd dropped it.

He smiled, grabbed the knife, and walked over in front of her. "Your mother's heart. Look. It's the last thing you'll ever see."

Then he smeared the bloody heart all over her face and neck and arms. Finally, he tossed it aside and came at her with the knife. At the first cut, she heard herself. The same sounds Mother had made were now coming from her.

The pain didn't end when the cutting stopped. Isabelle twisted in the grip of her captor, struggling to break free. Not because she thought she could escape. How could she? Her feet and hands were tied. And now she was blind.

Would she soon be dead?

Izzi jerked back to reality to find Galen watching her. "What's going on?" he asked.

293

"I'm not sure." That wasn't a lie. What she'd just experienced seemed genuine, but she couldn't be sure. She'd never remembered the song before, or the man in black dancing with her mother's body. So, what just happened here? Was there more than one killer? If so, why had she not remembered? Either she'd just reclaimed a forgotten memory, or someone had tried to put a memory into her head.

She'd bet on the first.

Izzi had always been convinced there were things about that night she'd forgotten. Whether her loss of memory was due to trauma or coercion from her monster, she didn't know. Maybe the how wasn't as important as the why. If she'd been made to forget, that would seem to indicate there was something about specific moments of that night that held the key to knowledge about her monster he didn't want to be known.

So, what significance did a child's song have to what happened?

"Isabelle?"

"What? Oh, sorry. I just – never mind it's not important." She looked around and saw Gib huddled with a group of men on the front porch of the house.

"What's going on?"

To his credit, Galen let the moment slide and answered her question. "The governor of Tennessee has already gone public to say the folks in Mississippi were wrong. The Seven Bridges Killer is not dead. Which means the case isn't closed."

"Just what he wanted."

"The killer?"

"Who else?"

Galen shrugged. "Anyone on this team. You. None of us want it to be closed."

"Are you sure about that?" She was interested in his perception of the team.

"Absolutely. It's in our blood now. The killer made it personal. To some of us, when Marty was killed. Then Leo nearly died. For the new people, when you were abducted and Gib almost died, it hit home."

"He made it personal," she murmured, then looked at him. "You're right. But what kind of advantage does it provide for him to have the case active?"

Galen shrugged. "Right off the top of my head? To get us where he wants us to be."

Within a blink, she was caught in a cold shiver that prompted her to grab her coat and put it on, then huddle up with her arms crossed and her shoulders up as she hunched into the warm fabric. She suddenly needed to talk to Gib. In private.

But that wasn't going to happen. Not for hours. So, she told herself to store the revelations and fears away, put them in a box, and close it. When they were finally alone, she'd open the box and reveal the awful truths to Gib.

For now, she'd go through the motions of viewing the crime. She got out of the vehicle and started to the house, walking beside Galen.

Did you ever see a lassie,
A lassie, a lassie,
Did you ever see a lassie,
Go this way and that?

Isabelle shivered and took Galen's arm. He gave her a questioning look but said nothing. Grateful for his silence and more for the insulation being in contact with him provided, she steeled herself for what they were about to witness.

Chapter Eighteen

Clarkesville, Tennessee

It'd been a long day, and by ten p.m., they were all
tired and frustrated. Forensics had netted no
evidence, material, or otherwise from the crime
scene. The BAU team met in one of the hotel
conference rooms where a small buffet had been set
up for them. That meant they could discuss the
investigation during dinner.

That grated on Izzi's nerves. She was obviously the
only person in the room who felt the need to take a
break from it now and again. Everyone knew it was
one of her peeves, so rarely did anyone ask her to
contribute during the dinner discussions. In fact,
there were times when she put in her earphones,
listened to music or an audiobook, or sometimes

read.

This evening her mind was occupied with the memory that returned today. She went over it time after time as she ate, trying to determine if it was real or something that had been planted in her mind. She prayed it was a real memory, as awful as that would sound should she speak it aloud. But if it was real, that meant someone else had made her forget and gave her a false narrative of her life that she took to be true.

She was more than a little unnerved by it but wasn't going to bring it up in front of the entire team. Only Gib could hear this truth.

"Hold on." Gib held up a hand, and the conversation, which had grown in volume over the last five minutes, silenced. He pulled out his phone and answered, "SAC Foster."

He looked around the room, and his gaze finally landed on Izzi as he said, "Thank you. Yes, we'll await your report."

Gib returned the phone to his jacket pocket. "A call came into the local PD about half an hour after we left the scene. A couple on the way home found something hanging from an old truss bridge. The man told police it looked like someone had thrown a hangman's noose over the truss. In the noose was a small burlap sack, soaked through with blood. The victim's heart and tongue were inside."

"And the girl?" Fiona asked.

"No sign of her. There's a bolo out for her statewide."

"Which means what for us?" Izzi asked.

"I'm not sure I understand the question."

"It's not complicated. Why are we even here? What good does it do? He kills and vanishes like a ghost, leaving us nothing to go on. The only thing we accomplish by being here is bolstering his ego."

Galen agreed, which pleased and surprised her. "It's his way of controlling us," he addressed the comment to Gib. "He wanted us to be here. The question is, why?"

"Do you know?" Gib asked Izzi.

"I wish I did, but no. I don't. I'm just..." She didn't feel she had the authority to finish the statement, so she just let it go and fell silent.

"You're just what?"

Izzi looked up at him, and he persisted. "What, Iz? Talk to us."

"Fine. I'm sorry. I guess I'm just tired. One the one hand, I just want a break from all this. It's like grime you can't wash off. But on the other hand, I can't step back. I'm just sick of being reactionary. That's what we are, you know. Already reacting to what he does. Chasing him. Letting him control the game."

"And you'd have us do what?" Leo asked. "Take control somehow?"

"Yes."

"And how would we accomplish that? How do we control the game if we can't find him?"

Here goes nothing, she thought and answered, "We set a trap."

"What kind of trap?" Dennis asked.

"The kind that will get his attention."

Gib leaned back in his chair and crossed his arms, an indication to her that while he would do her the courtesy of hearing her out, he still wasn't open to the idea.

"We'd need bait." It was the most straightforward answer she could compose.

"Bait?" Tamara blurted. "As in a person?"

"Yes." Izzi looked directly at Gib.

"And what bait, specifically, do you think would work?" His gaze bored into her with near tangible force.

"One of us."

A babble of voices erupted, and Izzi watched as Gib glared at her, then joined in the discussion.

She waited for over an hour, listening to everyone. Finally, Gib stood. "Listen, we're all tired, and there's nothing more we can do here except finishing up the reports. Fiona and Tamara have volunteered to stay on and take care of that. The rest of us will head back to Quantico in the morning.

"Everyone leaving tomorrow gets an extra two days added to their weekend. Fi? You and Tamara get two days added to your next weekend upon your return."

"Thanks," Fiona said gratefully and was echoed by Tamara.

"You've all earned it. Okay, that's it for me. Wheels up at nine in the morning, so we'll leave here at eight. Get some rest, everyone, and good work."

Galen rose and headed for the door but paused as he reached Izzi and leaned down to speak softly. "For what it's worth, I agree with you, but the chances of convincing Gib to go along with something like that are slim to none. He won't endanger his people."

"I wasn't talking about the BAU," she said just as softly and then turned so she could look at him. Their gazes met and held, and after a moment he nodded and straightened.

"See you in the morning, Isabelle."

"Yes. Rest well, Galen."

She stood and waited for Gib to walk over to her. "We need to talk," she said.

"Here?"

"No, my room."

"Then let's go."

Neither of them spoke again until they were in Izzi's room. She kicked off her shoes and sat on the bed. Gib remained standing. Having his hands in the pockets of his slacks and a slight rock from toes to heels made him appear impatient.

Or tired.

She understood that.

What they did made you tired in a way most people

don't understand. Seeing the darkness in humanity, the barbaric capacity – that weighed on you like a wet wool blanket. Heavy and suffocating. It wore you down, mentally, emotionally, and finally, physically.

Gib wasn't alone. Izzi recognized the signs of exhaustion in other members of the team. Which made it vital that he consider her suggestion without emotion or bias.

"Something happened." She knew that was a bad opening. He was in motion toward her before the final syllable left her lips.

"Are you all right?" He knelt on one knee in front of her.

"I am. I'm sorry, that was a poor choice of words. To be correct, I should have said I remembered something."

"You–you remembered something?"

She'd blame it on fatigue and frustration, that look that came into his eyes, the change in his expression. "Yes. About the killer."

Gib stood, turned, and sat beside her. "Tell me."

"When we arrived at the crime scene, I heard him singing, and it prompted a memory."

"What did he sing?"

"Do you remember a child's song that went, did you ever see a lassie, a lassie, a lassie?"

"Yes, my sisters sang it when they were on the swing-set as kids. He was singing that? Why?"

"Because that's what he sang to me the night my mother died."

"And you never remembered until today?"

"No."

"And I'm guessing there's more to it than simply remembering him singing?"

"Yes. He danced to it, holding my mother's dead body." Izzi tried not to let the mental image take shape in her mind again.

She could see the worry starting to turn his expression into a frown. "How can you be sure it's a memory, Iz? And if it is, what made you forget? Moreover, is it significant?"

"Yes, I know it's a memory because now I *do* remember. And it's significant because someone sang in my ear. Don't you get it? I saw the man in black, dancing with my mother's body, but someone had their hand tangled in my hair, kneeling on my back to keep me in place. And singing to me."

"A man?"

Suddenly she heard it again, so clear. "No. A boy."

"A boy? How old?"

Izzi closed her eyes, listening to the memory. "Teenager? Not grown. His voice hadn't deepened yet. It was a ... tenor. Sweet."

"Sweet?"

"The tone, not the monster."

"You mean there's a son of the monster?"

At those words, something slammed into her consciousness like a train. A big dark weight that snuffed out everything. Gib caught her as she toppled over, held, and shook her, patting her face. In a couple of seconds, she stiffened and gasped, "Oh my God. Gib, he's trying to rebuild his family."

"Are you telling me there's more than one?"

"There was."

She climbed back onto the bed and crossed her legs, Indian style. "I don't know if there still is, but I believe the one holding me was younger. His voice was younger."

Gib paced, stroking his mustache. "That would tie it up, you know. Explain how an adult man could start these killings in 1995 and keep them going for twenty-five years."

He stopped and looked at her. "He had an apprentice."

"So, who are we dealing with now?" she asked what she figured he was thinking. "The teacher or the student?"

"Or both?" Gib added. "Okay, we need to get the team on this as soon as we get back to Quantico, but until then, let's keep this between us."

"Okay."

"And Iz? I don't want to talk about setting traps right now. I know you're thinking you'd make perfect bait and you may be right, but I can't agree to that. Not now, and maybe not ever. I'm asking that you try and understand."

"I do," she said gently and held out her hand. "I couldn't bear putting you in harm's way, either."

"Then where does that leave us?" He took her hand and let her tug him toward the bed. Gib sat with his back propped against the headboard and pulled her up close to his side.

"I don't know," she said as she rested her head on his shoulder. "Honestly, I don't. I just want to stop him. I don't want him to be part of my world, and I know that's selfish, but I'm tired of being afraid and dreading the next time he whispers in my mind or the next time I hear him he's taken another life.

"This time –" she pulled back so she could look at him, "he has a little girl, Gib. An innocent child and –" She shook her head and looked away, unable to finish.

"And what, honey?"

Izzi shook her head again, but Gib persisted. "Don't clam up on me. What is it?"

"Tonight, while I was going over it in my head, more of the memories of that night returned. When they killed my mother and brother – after they cut my eyes, the boy kissed me and called me his special love. And I think maybe he touched me, raped me. I haven't remembered it happening, but I suspect it might have."

"And you didn't want me to know?"

"I didn't remember until now. They let me live, but they effectively destroyed my family, and my life would have been destroyed as well if I hadn't met Leo."

"Leo saved your life?"

"No. He opened the door for me to enter a world where monsters get stopped. Through him, I found you, and you saved my life."

"No, I didn't."

"Yes. Loving you saved me, Gib. You were the first person who made me want to learn how to stop my monster. I wanted you to like me, to be proud of me – to love me. You became the reason to keep going, and you still are. But I still feel guilty. I lived, and they didn't.

"And now he has another little girl. Only this one he didn't leave behind, and I'm terrified of what might happen to her. We have to find her. Using me as bait may be dangerous, but I'm willing to take the risk, and I'm begging that you give it consideration. We have to save her, Gib. We just have to."

He was quiet for a long time, and finally, he nodded. "I'll consider it. No guarantees, but I will give it fair consideration. That's all I can promise."

"That's enough. For now."

"Is it?"

"Yes."

She knew he wasn't just giving her lip service. He would honor his word and think about it.

"Do you want me to leave now so you can get some sleep?"

"No. I want you to get undressed and into bed with me. We'll tackle what to do tomorrow, but for now, let's take advantage of the time we have."

"You don't have to ask me twice." Izzi smiled, helped him undress, and then enjoyed the pleasure he delivered as he undressed her.

It didn't erase their problems or her concerns, but at least she could set those things aside for a little while and remind herself that she needed to celebrate and appreciate having Gib back in her life.

She knew now beyond all doubt that he was the one thing she never wanted to live without.

Chapter Nineteen

Quantico, Virginia

Izzi sat beside Galen, and Leo stood behind him as Galen called up the forensic report from the last crime scene. This was the last of the data, and the third time they'd reviewed it. Thus far, nothing new had jumped off the screen at any of them.

Galen pushed back from the desk and crossed his arms for a few moments, frowning at the screen. Then he looked at Izzi. "So, set a trap?"

"It seemed like a good idea when I said it."

"And now?"

"Now, I'm betting she's told Gib, and he said no," Leo answered the question.

"He wasn't a fan of the idea," she admitted.

"Then, what now?" Leo asked.

"Find that girl," Izzi said. "Is there any chance we can get our hands on something that belongs to her?"

"You think you can connect with her?" Leo asked.

"Honestly, probably not. My skills have never run in that direction, but I'm willing to try. We have to find her."

"How?" Galen asked

"I don't know." Izzi wished she did have an idea, some plan or suggestion. She'd done little but think about it since they left Tennessee. "By the way, when are Fi and Tamara due back?"

"Later this afternoon, I think," Leo replied, then frowned across the room.

Izzi turned her head at the same time Galen swiveled in his chair. Gib was just entering the room, and the expression on his face made a sick feeling take root in her stomach. He stopped and looked at them. "This morning, during shift change, a police officer reported that the officer posted outside Fiona and Tamara's room was not to be found in the hotel.

There was no answer when the office knocked on their door or when the hotel called the phone in the room, so the manager opened the door."

When his gaze locked on her, she knew it was bad, but nodded to let him know she could take whatever he had to say.

"Fiona was on the floor. Tied with articles of clothing and gagged. She'd been beaten badly, and a note was stapled to her chest."

"Stapled?" Leo blurted.

"Yes, but not an office stapler. A construction model that was taken from hotel maintenance."

"And the note said?" Galen asked.

"Game on."

Izzi barely made it out of her chair and to a trash can before vomiting. Leo took off out of the room as Gib hurried to her, grabbed her hair, and held it back from her face as she retched. By the time her stomach was empty, Leo was back with wet paper-towels in one hand and dry ones in the other.

"Thank you." She gratefully accepted both, cleaned herself up, dumped everything into the trash, and removed the plastic bag from the can. "Excuse me."

Izzi had to force herself to walk a normal pace to the restroom. She wanted to run. Once inside the bathroom, she stuffed the vile bag into the trash and set about rinsing her mouth and splashing water on her face. When the door opened, she whirled to see Gib enter, carrying her shoulder bag.

"Thank you." She took it, set it on the sink, and started rummaging through it. "Yes!" She pulled out the mini bottle of mouthwash she'd taken from the hotel.

"Old habits?" Gib asked as she opened it and filled her mouth.

She nodded, swished, gargled, spit, and rinsed. As she was drying her face, he walked over behind her and put his hands on top of her shoulders. "Want to tell me what just happened?"

"Game on." She looked up at him.

"The note?"

She nodded. "Where's Tamara?"

"We don't know."

"I do."

"Where?"

"He has her."

"You can't know that, Iz."

"But I do. In my gut, I know. She's first in the game." Izzi turned to face him. "He's going to kill her Gib, and it's going to be horrible. Now's the time for us to act. Turn his attention to me. Offer to make a trade. Something. We can't let him–" Thoughts of what he was capable of doing robbed her of breath, and she had to choke back a sob.

Gib pulled her into his arms. "We don't even know how to go about trying something like that."

"I do." She broke free, swiped at her eyes, and turned to snatch tissues from a container on the sink. "I know."

After blowing her nose and splashing water on her face again, she took a deep breath and looked up at his reflection in the mirror. "I know," she repeated, this time in control of her voice. "And before it's over, you're going to want me to use what I know how to do."

"You're just upset, and I understand, but–"

"No. I'm way beyond upset. I'm terrified, and you should be as well. Chances are Tamara is dead and – and she didn't die easy. He'll have made sure of that, just to make a point."

"Let's say you're right. What would provoke this? He's gotten away with his crimes for twenty-five years. Why take such a chance now? Killing an FBI agent will bring the full weight of the agency on him. Why would he want to open this can of worms?"

"Attention. Remember, he believes himself to be smarter than everyone else. He thinks he can manipulate and fool all of us. It's his game, and he believes, without doubt, he can win."

"What do you believe?"

"That he might be right unless we make up our mind to beat him at his own game."

"And put your head on the chopping block."

"No. Don't forget, he had me once. For three months. He hurt me, terrified me, and nearly broke me mentally, but he never once tried to kill me. It's not my head he wants, Gib. It's my heart."

"As in on a plate."

"Maybe. But even if that's the case, it may be a risk we need to take."

"Well, I won't, and I'm not discussing it further, so if you're okay–"

"I am."

She marched by him and out of the door. She didn't

wait for him but hurried back to where Leo and Galen waited. Dennis was there as well. "Has anyone spoken with Fiona? What are the extent of her injuries? Is there video surveillance in the hotel, and if so, can we get our hands on the footage from last night? Has anyone-"

"Whoa, slow down there, hotshot." Galen was the one to interrupt.

"Excuse me?" She threw one hand on a hip and glared at him, not angry with him, just the situation in general. She was actively working on being angry. The madder she was, the less afraid and sick she would feel. And the less chance *he* would have to get inside her head.

Just then, Gib walked back into the room. "Okay, people, wheels up in two hours. There's an APB out for Tamara, and as soon as Fiona is conscious, we'll question her. The local PD has the footage from hotel security and is forwarding us a copy. Dennis, be ready to retrieve it inflight, so we can have a look before we land. Questions?"

No one spoke, so Gib nodded. "Then let's get moving."

It took less than a minute for the room to clear, leaving Izzi standing on one side and Gib on the other, looking at one another. "For the record, I always place value on what you say, Iz, and always consider your suggestions, but for the last time, I don't know that you'll ever convince me that making you bait for this psychopath is a good idea."

"It's okay." She started across the room. "I don't know that it ever will be a *good* idea. I just think it might end up being the only idea that has a chance of putting us in the same room with him."

"Maybe," he replied and placed his hand on the side of her face as she stopped in front of him. "I love you, Iz. The idea of putting you in danger– it does something to me. Something bad."

"I understand. Let's not talk about that anymore. Let's focus on Fiona and hopefully finding Tamara."

He nodded, pivoted, and gestured toward the door. "You think we have a chance of finding her?"

"Yes."

"Just yes?"

Izzi nodded and said no more. He wouldn't have wanted to hear it anyway. She did believe they'd find Tamara. But not alive. Her monster wouldn't take a chance on leaving Tamara alive. Not a trained agent, who might just pick up on something she could use to identify him.

No. He wouldn't take that chance.

Besides, he'd already told them. He was after them. Which meant he intended to kill every single one of them. Until there was no one left but him and her.

Izzi grit her teeth as she accompanied Gib out of the building. She'd be damned if she'd let her monster kill this team. She was going to stop him. End him. Or die trying.

In Route to Clarksville, Tennessee

Everyone gathered around Dennis as he played the footage obtained from hotel security. The timestamp showed the first change in the shift for an officer to be posted outside the doors to Fiona and Tamara's rooms. The officer took a seat, pulled out his phone, and diddled with it. There was no activity at all in the hallway outside of their rooms. Not until an hour before shift change.

The office on duty looked up toward the elevator and, after a moment, looked back down at his phone in his hand. Ten minutes later, he looked up again, but this time got up and walked toward the camera.

After a slight glitch in the video, it resumed to show the officer walking toward the chair placed along the wall between the hotel doors. He took a seat and pulled out his cell phone. From that point on, there was nothing to see for hours except the officer paying attention to his phone. Near time for a change in shift, there was another glitch, and when the video became clear again, EMT and police were entering the hotel rooms. There was no sign of the original officer on duty.

Dennis fast-forwarded to the end of the recording. Even though video footage from the lobby showed EMTs and police entering, nothing showed the officer on duty leaving.

"Can you rewind that a bit?" Izzi asked. She thought she noticed something odd but wanted to make sure.

"Sure, how far?"

"First, look at the officer when he first arrives and takes a seat."

Dennis rewound, and they watched the footage. "Okay, and?" Dennis asked.

"Is there any way for you to clip that section and display it in a window of its own?"

"Absolutely." It took him under a minute. "Now what?"

"Now go to where he gets up, walks toward the

camera, and disappears, then returns."

She watched the video fast-forward until the officer came into frame with his back to the camera. "Okay, clip that section until he takes a seat and takes out his phone."

Dennis did as she asked. "What are we looking for?"

"Is there a way to tell if these clips are identical?"

Galen looked at her. "What are you thinking?"

"You know what I'm thinking. The video has been altered."

"Can we play them simultaneously?" Gib asked.

"Yes!"

Dennis' fingers flew over the keyboard, copying and pasting the clips from the original footage and putting them into a new timeline, stacked one atop the other. "The top video is the last one on the recording. I'm making it 70 percent transparent and color-correcting it to green so we can see if there's a difference."

It took about five minutes to get the starting point correct, but once he accomplished that and played the clip, it was obvious. The two clips were identical.

"How is this possible?" Gib asked.

Dennis shook his head, pursed his lips, and stared at the screen for a few moments. "It stands to reason that this entire section of video has been tampered with, so there should be something to prove it, some mistake or--"

Izzi interrupted, "Check the movements of the officer. Do they repeat at all?"

Within minutes they all saw it. The officer's movements did, in fact, repeat. Several times. "And the time codes." Izzi pointed to the bottom of the footage. "Look at the point when he shifts in his seat and coughs."

Dennis ran the tape in slow motion. "There!" Galen pointed. "The counter on the seconds backed up from zero six to zero five."

"So, what does all this tell us?" Leo, who until then had been silent, asked.

"That he did all this right under our noses," Dennis answered. "He'd have to have been in the hotel and have access to the surveillance videos to make the changes and replace the originals with the doctored versions."

"And he'd have to have done it quickly," Galen

added. "In order to have time to kill the officer on duty before his replacement arrived, beat up Fiona, and take Tamara."

"So, you're saying he was there the whole time?" Leo asked.

Galen looked at Izzi. "What do you think?"

"I think he was."

"Then here's the million-dollar question," Leo responded. "Why?"

"Game on," she said, reciting the words on the grizzly note he'd left them. "He wanted us to find this and figure it out."

"Because?" Dennis asked.

"To remind us that he's smarter," Galen looked at Izzi as he answered.

"Yes," she agreed.

"Then we're just going to have to prove him wrong," Galen said and stood. "I don't know about the rest of you, but I've about had it with this bastard. I think it's time to put him in the ground."

"You'll get no argument from me," Leo agreed.

"I think that's what we'd all like," Gib said calmly. "But that's not our way. We'll find him, and we'll put him behind bars."

"Or death row," Dennis offered.

"Works for me," Leo remarked.

Izzi didn't comment or join the conversation. She didn't believe they stood a chance of catching her monster. None of them would ever get close to him unless he wanted them to. Which meant she had to find a way to convince Gib that their plan had to be to give the monster what he wanted.

How she'd accomplish that was a mystery. But for the sake of the members of the team still alive, she had to try.

Chapter Twenty

Clarksville, Tennessee

Gib couldn't remember feeling as exhausted, beaten down, or heartsick as he did right now. He lay in bed, staring at the ceiling. Izzi lay beside him with her head on his shoulder and one arm across his body.

He knew she wasn't sleeping and would have been surprised if she was. They'd visited with Fiona at the hospital, and it was difficult to see how badly she'd been hurt and how much pain she was in. The doctors had already informed her she would require several surgeries to rebuild her nose and one cheekbone and insert dental implants to replace all the teeth missing. There was a chance her left leg would be permanently handicapped.

Gib wanted to hit something, shoot something, do

some damage to get this rage out of his gut. No, that wasn't true. He wanted to hurt the killer. As bad or more than he'd hurt Fiona. Gib wanted to make the man suffer.

He wanted something to erase the feeling of helplessness. He'd been there once before and was pretty sure the only reason he survived was Izzi. It was at that moment he realized he'd never told her.

"Are you asleep?" He knew full well she was not.

He felt her shift and moved a bit as well, so he could look at her. "Do you remember when I showed up at your house a month after Diana died?"

She kissed his chest and then responded, "I've never seen anyone more broken."

Broken. That was an apt description. Gib didn't allow himself to revisit that time much. There was still a lot of pain and grief. At the moment, however, he was taken back in time without warning.

He didn't much remember the trip, or even making a conscious decision to make it. He was standing in the bedroom he'd shared with his wife, looking at her clothing he'd taken from the closet and dresser. Her things lay on the bed like they were alive, daring him to touch or dispose of them. If he did, was he disposing of her? Of them and what they'd shared?

Gib wasn't sure what to do anymore. His children had come to terms with their mother's death and were starting to reclaim their lives. Diana hadn't suffered. At least according to the doctors. She was playing tennis with her best friend and just fell, dead before she landed.

An aneurysm in her brain burst, killing her nearly instantly.

Still, he couldn't help but ask and wonder. What were her last thoughts? Did she have time to understand what was happening? Was there pain? God, he didn't even have a chance to say goodbye, to thank her for all the love she'd given him, all she'd done for their family.

And worst of all, he'd never come clean and confessed that while he loved her more than he could ever say, he'd given a piece of his heart to a young woman she'd come to think of as a daughter. Would he ever live down that guilt? If Diana was here now, would she forgive him if he confessed?

Suddenly the walls all seemed to close in at once, and he felt like he couldn't breathe. He didn't think about it, didn't plan, he just got in his car and started driving.

Now, here he was, standing at Izzi's front door. It opened, and she took one look at him before stepping forward and wrapping her arms around his waist to hug him tight.

That's when the tears came. Tears he'd held back for months. Tears he'd been ashamed or afraid to shed. But with Izzi, he could, and so he let it all out, quietly standing on her front porch, hanging onto her and feeling her hold him.

He arrived broken.

When he left two weeks later, the cracks were starting to heal. Six months later, he returned, and that time, when he left, she accompanied him.

"You healed me, Iz. You accepted my love for Diana, and my kids as well. They never felt they had to put their love for their mother in a closet when you were around. You helped me, and the kids celebrate the life we had with her and made us realize how much you loved her as well. Because of you, we were able to share that with one another. I'll never be able to repay what you did for me. For all of us. Thank you. I know that it will never be enough, but I will feel it every day. Just like I'll love you every day I live."

It didn't happen often, but every now and then, Izzi's emotions broadcast strongly enough that people around her could feel them. He did now. He felt the depth of her love and knew it to be true and enduring. She didn't measure his love for her against what he had and still felt for Diana, or his children. She simply accepted what he gave with sincere gratitude and returned it ten-fold.

"God, I'm so lucky to have you in my life, Iz."

"Not half as lucky as –"

The way her body stiffened, her breath hitched, and her words cut off abruptly, scared him. Gib sat, pulling her upright. "What's wrong? Iz, what is it?"

Her eyes were open, white, and unblinking, letting him know she was seeing something no one else could, and it was likely to be bad. Gib knew better than to try and pull her out of whatever she was experiencing, so he just held onto her and watched.

Izzi struggled against the ropes binding her wrists and the hands tangled in her hair, preventing her from moving her head. A face came into view, someone looking down at her.

The hands were holding one of her eyelids closed while something cold and wet dripped on it.

Then her eyelid was pried open wide and pressed back against the skin behind her eye. She wanted to squint her eye closed, but it was held firm.

All she could do was try not to scream.

When the hands moved away, she quickly tried to close both eyes. That's when the scream erupted. She could only close one eye. What had been done to her?

The laughter told her that her fear and discomfort was a source of pleasure, and it made her mad.

Why would anyone do such an awful thing?

She struggled harder, desperate to break free as the process was done to her other eye.

Within minutes, the attention was on Donny, doing the same thing to him.

Gluing his eyes open. It was awful. Like a nightmare.

And it only got worse.

As Donny was held in place, so was she.

That's when she realized. The monster who was hurting her mother was not alone.

"No!" She screamed and fought to get away, retching and crying as she witnessed the carnage.

And suddenly, in the space of a heartbeat, the scene

shifted. She was no longer in her room, being held by an unseen captor, made to witness her mother being brutalized.

Now she saw it happen to Tamara, and the eyes she looked through were not her own. She felt the scream rising in her throat as she watched the monster cut out Tamara's tongue and toss it aside.

Small hands held Tamara's face, unsuccessful in preventing Tamara from turning her head side to side as she struggled to raise her head. She fought the darkness that loomed over her, casting a shadow on her and the pale child with bandaged eyes who knelt behind her head.

Izzi's terror released the scream in accompaniment to the voice of her monster. *I'll leave her pieces where you can find them, my love. I'll let you know when I've finished.*

Izzi mentally recoiled, screaming and reaching blindly. "Gib!"

Gib had her in his arms, holding her tight the moment his name burst from her lips. "I've got you. I've got you. You're safe. I'm here, Iz. You're safe."

She clung to him, trembling like someone who had just been pulled from freezing water. It shocked him to realize her skin felt like it.

Gib grabbed the blanket and wrapped it around them, pulling her onto his lap so that her legs circled his waist and her body was pressed around his. Within moments he felt the heat leaching out of his own body and into hers. A few seconds passed, and suddenly warmth suffused her and then him.

Izzi pulled back to look at him, and he saw tears streaming down her face.

"Tell me." His hands moved to cup her face gently.

"Tamara," she whispered brokenly.

"Tell me what you saw?"

Izzi hesitated. She wouldn't outright lie to Gib, but there were things she'd seen – memories that had surfaced – that provided information previously hidden. It was information she wasn't sure about just yet. Not it's veracity, but what to do with it. She needed to sink deeper into her own memories and see if she could drag out other things that had been hidden.

And Gib wanted answers to what was happening now, not what happened in the past. She could tell him what she'd been shown, as awful as it was.

"He showed me. He's making the child help, Gib. Making her participate in –" She stopped and choked back tears.

"He said he'd leave her pieces where we can find them and will let me know when he's finished."

"Dear God." Horror was evident on his face. "What the hell do we do? We have to stop him, Iz."

It was the question she'd been waiting on. "Then we have to stop being pawns in the game. He's made his opening move. It's time we make ours."

"And do what?"

"You know what. We offer him a trade. Me for the girl."

"What makes you think he'll go for it?"

Izzi didn't hold back and was honest with Gib in her answer. "I'm not sure he would go through with a trade, but I'd bet the farm that he'd pretend to go along with it, just to get us in the same place."

"We're back to that? Using you as bait?"

"Well, what would you prefer, Gib? That we start making a habit of literally picking up the pieces of your team after he slaughters them?"

She could tell her words were the mental equivalent of a slap and felt terrible for being so blunt. Still, she needed him to understand the severity of the situation. He was, right now, brutally murdering Tamara, and she was just the beginning. If they didn't do something to catch him, he would not stop until they were all dead.

And she was once more his prisoner.

Gib was silent for a long time, so long she started to slide off his lap. But his hands wrapped around her upper arms and stopped her. "If we do this, I'm going to be with you every second. You won't be allowed out of my sight. And we have to make sure whatever location we choose, it has state of the art surveillance."

"Okay but-"

"Let me finish, in addition, agents will be clandestinely posted to keep watch. They'll be on a two-minute response time if we call on them."

Izzi waited for a beat, then responded. "One provision."

"What's that?"

"That we don't tell the rest of the team."

"Why?"

She could tell the truth without revealing things she

needed to keep hidden a while longer. "Because I think he's somehow in contact and knows what goes on with us. We can't let anyone on our team know this plan."

He nodded. "Then I'll put them to work clearing everyone, anyone any of us have come into contact with."

"That will take a while."

"Exactly. And while they are doing that, we will be on a short leave of absence."

"Where?"

"We won't tell anyone until we're in place."

"Okay, can I make a suggestion?"

"Yes, of course."

"My house. It's remote enough he'd feel secure trying to take me there, and due to its remoteness, not likely for anyone to notice if we have the surveillance set up in advance. I can make a point of letting it be known in advance that I'm having some work done to the place – upgrading old wiring and plumbing, that sort of thing."

"That's a good idea."

She nodded."Then, we have the beginning of a plan?"

"We do."

Izzi hugged him, holding on tight. She had to figure out the truth of what happened the night her mother and brother were killed, dig out the memories that had been buried. There was power in that knowledge, a power she might well need to stand a chance of defeating her monster.

And this time, when she faced him, she *had* to defeat him. If she couldn't use her abilities to drag him out of the darkness and into the light where his evil could not survive, then she had to be willing to put an end to him in a way Gib would probably hate, but would nonetheless support.

She had to be willing to kill him.

Chapter Twenty-One

Concord, North Carolina

Izzi had never feared storms. Just the opposite. She marveled at the power of nature and felt humbled by it. Storms reminded her of just how powerless humans were in comparison to nature.

Plus, she loved the sound of rain on the roof, the rumble of thunder, and the sound of wind in the trees. Storms were a time to snuggle up in a warm place, sip a good cup of tea, or perhaps a cup of tea laced with a shot of whiskey, and relax.

She felt the coming of the storm just before dusk. With it came an unexpected wave of anxiety. Izzi stepped out onto the back porch, looked around, and sniffed the air. There was an unusual energy tonight, and it wasn't from the approaching storm.

Gib walked out of the house and stood beside her. "Everything okay?"

"I don't know. There's something…I don't know – something."

"The storm, maybe?"

"No, not the storm."

"Him?" Gib put his arm around her shoulders and snuggled her into his side. She could feel his holstered weapon pressing against her, reminding her how much she hated this situation.

She looked up at him and then out at the gathering darkness. "I don't know."

"Well, if he comes, we're ready."

"We've been ready for two weeks." She knew he was as tired of the wait as she. For the first few days, they both jumped at every creak of the house. Now they were just frustrated. "Maybe he knows."

"He couldn't. We were too careful."

Izzi knew he wanted to think they were. She did, too. But the truth was, she didn't trust anyone aside from Gib, and she believed if there was a way to ferret out the information on what they were doing, her monster would find that way. However, now wasn't the time to argue that point with Gib. They were both tense and restless, waiting for something to happen while being filled with dread.

"I love you, Gib."

He turned her to face him. "I love you, Iz. We'll make it through this."

"I hope so. I've wished for so long that you and I–" She couldn't finish the sentence. Her throat constricted, and she was suddenly cold.

Hello, my love.

I'm sorry to make you wait so long.

And I know you've been waiting for me.

Do you remember our first time?

You cried so pretty. I licked those tears, sang to you as I loved you.

Do you remember?

Izzi sucked in a breath, like someone rising from beneath the waves, desperate for air. In her head, his voice crooned.

So never leave me lonely. Tell me you love me only. And that you'll always... let it be me.

"Gib!" Her hands clutched at him even as her legs gave way. Hearing that song was like someone setting off an explosive charge in her mind that shook the foundations of her consciousness, dislodging the blockages that barred her from remembering.

She was so close. Images danced and swam in a mix of fast and lazy currents, almost within reach.

Almost.

Can you see clearly now, my love?

Izzi moaned, unaware that she'd made a sound. Her monster was there, and his question was the missing piece, the key that finally unlocked all the memories that had been hidden.

At last, the door was open. All she had to do was step through.

Even with the urgency to take the step pulling at her, she was aware of the danger. Once she crossed that threshold, she might never emerge. She had to consider that it might be a cunning trap. Entice her with the memories she so desperately wanted to recover and trap her within her own mind.

Are you strong enough?

His question was an echo from the past. He'd asked

her that before and tonight her answer was the same it had been all those years ago when she was but seven years old and terrified by the carnage she'd been forced to witness.

I will destroy you.

She heard the steel in her own astral voice and the sound of his chuckle.

That's my girl.

Then a maelstrom claimed her, and she was catapulted back in time, like Dorothy, spinning through a tornado. Only she wasn't unceremoniously dumped in a strange land. No, indeed. Her landscape was all too familiar.

And all too terrifying.

"Look, Izzi, look!"

Izzi sometimes hated those words. Donny always wanted her to watch him play, see him make his character on the video game jump or run. She usually would make a polite comment, praise him for his skills, or just smile and say, "Way to go!" But sometimes, she wished he would just let her play with her cards and not have to pay attention to him.

Like tonight. She was so close to winning. Her dad had taught her to play solitaire last year when she was six, and it'd taken her a whole year to get good at the game. Still, she couldn't hurt Donny's feelings, so she looked at the television and then smiled at him. "Wow, you're really getting good."

His smile made her glad she'd been kind. Just like her Grandpa always said, "If you can choose to be anything, be kind."

Izzi heard voices from the kitchen and frowned. Her mama had a visitor, and Izzy didn't much like it. Why would Mama invite a man over to their home while Daddy was away?

Izzi didn't even know who the man was, but her mama had put on one of her nice dresses and fixed her hair and put on makeup and everything.

She thought about going into the kitchen but decided against it. Her mama told her to stay in the room with Donny, and Izzi didn't want to get into trouble, so she turned her attention back to her card game.

It wasn't until she heard an odd sound at the door to the bedroom that she realized the voices had stopped. Izzi looked toward the door, and at that moment, her mother was sort of pushed through the opening.

A man dressed all in black, with gloves covering his hands and a tight black mask that covered his face and head, had hold of her mama. One of his gloved hands was tangled in her hair, and the other held a knife to her neck, the knife her dad used to clean fish they caught at Miller's pond.

Fear made her heart jump in her chest and sweat break out all over her. Izzi didn't know what to do except scoot over to Donny and put herself in front of him. The man in black laughed, and it sounded strange. He pushed Izzi's mother further into the room, and that's when another surprise was delivered.

Two teenage boys entered with the man in black. Two beautiful boys, at least to Izzi's eyes. They hurried over to her and Donny, smiling like they were friends.

They most certainly were not. They were the children of the monster.

The realization jolted Izzi from the memory. How could she have forgotten? Not just the truth of that night when her mother was murdered, but the truth of what she'd learned when she was kidnapped and held prisoner.

There *were* two boys there on the night her mother was killed. Twins. Identical twins. They were learning from their father. Not their real father, but

342

the man who took them from one of his kills when they were six years old. They became children of the killer the night he butchered their mother.

He'd only wanted one of them to replace the son he killed the night he murdered his own wife, but one of the boys was clever. Clever enough to convince the man to take them both. Over the course of time, that clever boy, the only one who was given a name, learned to manipulate the father while he and his twin learned all they could.

By the time they showed up at Izzi's house, they were far more skilled than the man who had mentored them, and a lot smarter. The night their father killed Izzi's mother, they killed him and made it look like an accident. They went to live with an elderly aunt who never caught on that there were actually two of them. When the time came, they killed her too, inherited what she had, and started a life of their own – two young men with one name.

Her legs nearly gave way beneath her. Gib supported her and led her back inside the house. "Honey, what is it?"

"Gib, I know. I know the truth now."

"What truth?" He guided her through the kitchen and toward the sitting room.

"About the night my mother and Donny died. About my monster. He isn't what–" She sensed her monster a split second too late.

Gib was also a second too late in drawing his weapon. Izzi screamed and tried to push him out of the way but was unsuccessful. She saw a glint of light off the blade and heard a harsh grunt from Gib. He staggered and then grunted again.

Izzi heard the blade cut through clothing and flesh and whirled around, lashing out in hopes of hitting her monster. Her fists met only emptiness. She turned back toward Gib. He was panting and trying, unsuccessfully, to draw his weapon.

She wrapped one arm around his waist. "Hold onto me."

It's over, Isabelle.

I win. If you surrender now, I'll let him live.

God, how she hated that voice, how she hated him. If only she could stop shaking. Fear was as much her enemy as he. Yet, she couldn't blame it all on him. This was a trap of her own design, one that had, unfortunately, not unfolded as planned. Every creak of wood, drip of water, or brush of leaves against a window made her heart jump in her chest.

344

She helped Gib into the house and across the room, away from the door. Izzi eased him to the floor, propped against the wall. His breath was labored, and when she moved her hands from where she'd been holding onto him, they came away wet with his blood.

She rose just enough to peer from behind the curtain of the window.

She didn't see movement outside, but it was a cloudy night, and without the light from the moon, the yard was cast in grey on black, indistinct shapes and varying degrees of darkness that shifted in the wind of the approaching storm.

At her feet lay the man she loved, the man who had already nearly died once trying to save her from her monster. Now his life was at risk again.

The deepest of the stab wounds in his upper back had luckily missed his lung, but she was worried that the second might be affecting his kidney.

The third, the one in his shoulder, didn't appear to have hit any major arteries but was bleeding profusely. The shoulder wound had obviously done more damage than she could see because he couldn't raise his arm or grip. Which meant he couldn't use his gun.

Izzi rushed to find the first aid kit under the kitchen sink. There was tape and gauze in it. She used what she had and snatched dish towels from a drawer to bind the wounds.

She snatched up the landline. Dead. Then she tried turning on the back porch light. Nothing happened. Had he done something to kill the electricity to the house? With the power shut down, no internet or cell reception, they were cut off. If he was going to survive, she had to get them out of there.

The problem was, Isabelle didn't know how. The moment she opened the door, they'd be vulnerable to attack, and she was sure the monster would kill Gib this time. She couldn't let that happen, but she had no weapons. She didn't know how to fire Gib's gun, and even if he told her, she probably couldn't hit the broad side of a barn.

Isabelle, I'm waiting for you.

Come to me, my love.

Don't make me kill him.

Come to me, and he lives. Just take that step, Isabelle. Cross the last bridge that will bring you forever to me.

The bridge. That phrase brought another rush of

memories that weakened her mentally and physically. She sank back down and whispered to Gib, "Maybe if I go outside–"

"No."

She put her fingertips to his lips. "Listen to me. I'm not going to let him kill you, and you know he doesn't want me dead, so this is the best way. I'll make a deal with him. I make him call for an ambulance, and then I'll go with him."

"So he can put you back inside a cage? Iz, don't. We'll fight him together. Just take my gun."

"Gi–"

"No, you listen. Take my gun and do exactly as I say. You can do this."

For a split second, she hesitated. The part of her that was terrified to lose him said to just leave him there. Leave him and go make a deal with the devil so Gib could live.

The part that was trying not to scream in terror at the idea of being a prisoner to the monster told her to take the chance. If she killed him, it was over. They were free, and the long nightmare was over.

"Do it, Iz.

"For us. Let's end this. End him."

"Yes," she agreed, letting herself succumb to her own darkness and need for the terror to end. "Yes. Tell me what to do."

Within moments they were ready. She was ready. For the first time in her life, she willingly opened herself, allowing the evil to hear her.

I have to see you. Come inside.

She waited, trembling and feeling her hands grow wet with sweat. The gun felt too heavy, too big. If he came in, could she pull the trigger? Could she hit him?

Isabelle watched the door until she was nearly blind, until everything seemed to merge into a featureless blur of shadow. When the door handle moved, making a slight click, she almost wet her pants.

The door opened, and a darker form within the gray moved across the threshold. Two more steps, and light from the window to her left slanted across a tall figure. Beside him was a small figure, whose hand was in the grip of the monster. And holding her other hand was the monster's twin. All the air went out of Isabelle's lungs and she nearly dropped the gun.

"Oh, dear God."

"Shoot, Iz," Gib panted the words, every moment, every breath an effort.

Come, her monster urged. *I promise I'll let him live. I'll let them both live.*

"Iz, shoot!"

"I said come!" the monster's twin roared, this time not merely in her head.

Isabelle screamed, raised the weapon, and pulled the trigger. It flashed brightly in the darkness, making spots of light dance in her vision, and the rapport of the gun made it impossible to hear.

She felt someone grab her, trying to take the gun, and she pulled the trigger again. It sounded like another weapon fired as well, but she couldn't be sure because, in a flash, the world exploded into an endless sea of white.

That's when she saw it, the memory that had been hidden from her. She remembered now.
Remembered them holding her down while they took turns raping her. The one who delighted in causing pain laughed with delight. The other whispered to her that she just had to relax. They were making her belong to them.

It wasn't just that once. They took her from her

grandparents' home when she was eleven and again when she was fourteen.

Izzi remembered waking up on the back porch of her grandparents' home, being scolded about running off for days and told what a horrible child she was.

Yes, now she remembered. Being their prisoner. The twin with no name wanted to cause her pain. The other one let him, but never allowed him to cause permanent damage.

And the one who didn't torture, removed the pain and fear. His touch insulated her from that. It was how she'd survived. By depending on his touch to keep her sane.

She remembered now. They were both insane, but in different ways. The one with the name liked to see if he could outsmart everyone. And he planned the murders to keep his twin under control. If he didn't, there was no telling what his twin might do.

"I know you now." She raised the gun and pointed it at the one who made the decisions, the one who had a name.

He didn't seem at all afraid. "You're not a good shot, love," he chuckled and then continued. "Well, Isabelle, what is the answer? After all these years and all that's passed between us. You said that first night that you'd never forgive us. Never love us. Maybe God would, but not you. Is that true or merely something you cling to because you don't want to admit that you forgave us long ago. The first time we took you. When you were eleven, and your grandparents thought you'd run away. And remember when you were fourteen? You were far more ready then.

"Not as passionate as you were a few years ago, though. Ah, yes, I see from your expression you remember now."

"Oh, I remember, Galen. I remember it all."

"Galen?" Gib struggled to sit upright. "Where's Galen? Iz, what's going in?"

"Don't Gib. Save your strength. Please."

Izzi kept her eye on the man who'd made her life hell. More correctly, at one of the men. She wasn't sure which of them she hated more.

"Maybe the truth is, you've loved us all along." His taunt interrupted her thoughts. "You just couldn't admit it."

"Not a chance," she insisted. "My answer is still the same. I'll never forgive you."

"But God might."

"Maybe. But I'm not God."

And then she pulled the trigger. Three times in quick succession. The one who had a name let go of the girl and ran. The other stumbled, reached for the doorframe for support, and then fell, pulling the child down with him.

Izzi heard sirens. She turned to check Gib. He was unconscious but breathing. She stood and hurried across the room. "Hello, sweetheart," she said to the child. "My name's Isabelle. I won't hurt you."

"He will."

"Not anymore," Izzi said and reached out to touch the little girl.

The child flinched and then dove into Izzi's arms, trembling and sobbing softly. Izzi held her close, then stood with the child wrapped around her body. She looked down at the man on the floor. Even in the waning light, she could see the blood that stained his shirt. Two of the bullets had found their mark, one in the center of his chest and the other in his lower abdomen. He wouldn't survive long.

"You shot the wrong one, Isabelle," the monster panted the words. "He'll continue to kill, you know. And he'll keep coming after you. After all of you. He'll plan the perfect, horrible end for each of you."

"Will he? He's never killed anyone. He plans it all for you, videos what you do, and yes, takes pleasure in watching it happen, but he's never killed. You're the one who likes to torture and cause pain. You're the real killer."

"We're the real killer. He and I. We're one and the same. Don't you know that by now?"

"I know all of it. I remember everything, you psycho. You're both insane and deserve to rot in hell. I'm betting you will, both of you, but you're going to get there first. And he won't get away. There's nowhere he can hide now that we know who he is. But you? You won't last five more minutes."

"I'd like to slit your throat."

"Not going to happen," she said and then jumped slightly at the sound of a voice in her comm unit. It was Leo.

"We're here, Izzie. We're here. Are you okay?"

"Gib needs help now. Please hurry."

She ignored the dying man on the floor and carried the child back to where Gib lay on the floor.

"Sit right here, sweet girl," she said as she sat and placed the child on the floor beside her. The little girl wrapped herself around Izzi's side, hanging on tight and still shaking.

"It's okay," Izzi tried to assure her. "You're safe now. I just need to check on my friend, okay?'

"Okay." The girl's response was barely above a whisper.

Izzi put her hand on the side of Gib's face. "Gib? Can you hear me? Gib?"

"Iz?"

"Help is here. Just hang on. We're safe now."

She wasn't sure she fully believed that, but it was important that he feel safe. Seconds later, the yard was awash in lights, flashing red, blue, and white. Leo was the first one in the door and tripped over the monster on the floor.

"Oh my god, is that–?"

"No," Izzi interrupted. "It's his twin."

"Dear God."

Leo hurried to her and knelt beside Gib.

"Hey, buddy, the medics are coming in the door now. Hang on, you hear?"

"I'm not going anywhere." Gib's voice was weak but determined.

Leo smiled, put his hand on Gib's shoulder, and then looked at Izzi. "Who shot him?"

"I did."

"Izzi, this twin thing."

"I'll explain it all, I promise." She stood as the medics reached them and stepped out of their way.

As soon as they had Gib loaded onto a gurney and were headed for the door, she fell in behind them and followed them to the ambulance. "We have to go with him. And this child needs medical attention."

No one argued, for which she was grateful. Within minutes she was sitting beside Gib, holding his hand as the child clung to her.

"What happened to the child?" one of the medics asked.

"Her eyes were cut."

"Good god."

He activated his radio to communicate to the hospital that along with a gunshot victim they had a child with eye trauma coming in.

"Thank you," Izzi said.

"You bet."

"Iz?"

Gib opened his eyes. "Are you okay?"

"I am. We're safe now."

"And the Unsub?"

The last thing she wanted to do was lie, but this wasn't the place or time to try to explain it to him, so she fibbed a bit. "I shot him."

"Dead?"

"I don't know." That part was correct. She had no clue if the monster was still alive. The awful part was she almost hoped not, although if he lived, it might give them a better chance of finding his twin.

That revelation was going to hit everyone hard, and she dreaded having to explain. But she'd face that when the time came.

Right now, all she cared about was Gib surviving and getting help for the child.

Everything else could wait.

Chapter Twenty-Three

Six Months Later
Concord, NC

"He looks like a cowboy," Alex said, which caused Izzi to look up from the task of pulling radishes out of the ground.

"Ha, you're right." She leaned over to give Alex a one-armed hug, then raised her arm to wave at Gib as he walked toward them.

Dressed in faded jeans, a button-down shirt with the sleeves rolled up, and a straw cowboy hat, he did indeed look like one of those handsome cowboys on the pages of a magazine. She smiled and thought about how blessed she was to have a life with him.

He and Alex. Since Alex's family was dead, Gib

pulled some strings, and Izzi adopted the child. She was as sweet as the day was long and had not complained at all about the three surgeries required to restore her vision.

The only complaint she had was that she'd wanted her eyes to be like Izzi's.

Izzi hadn't known she wanted a child until Alex was thrust into her life. Now she couldn't imagine life without the child. Or without Gib. While he'd said upfront that he didn't want to raise another child, his stance had changed. Now Alex was the little sister his grown children doted on, and the little girl who idolized him.

It was more than Izzi had hoped for, and she counted her blessings daily. Her only concern was that Alex was more like her than anyone realized. Izzi could sense the child's awakening abilities and tried daily to guide her on how to deal with them.

"Well, don't you two look happy as pigs in mud," Gib said as he squatted down beside Izzi and reached out to ruffle Alex's hair.

"Are pigs happy in mud?" Alex asked.

"To tell you the truth, I don't know," Gib admitted.

Izzi's laugh was cut short. Two things happened

simultaneously. Alex's head popped up, neck straight and stretched up like a little rabbit catching the scent of a predator. And a voice sounded in Izzi's mind.

Have you missed me?

Izzi brushed off her hands, smiled at Gib, and gathered up her tools and basket. "How about we go inside and fix ice cream cones?"

Alex looked up at her with a puzzled look on her face, and Izzy gestured. "Grab your stuff, girlie, and let's get to that ice cream."

"Yes, ma'am. Want me to put your tools in the potting shed?"

"That'd be very nice. Thank you, Alex."

"She goes out of her way to be helpful," Gib commented as Alex dashed off with the garden tools.

"We're not alone." Izzi hated to announce it so abruptly, but there was no time to beat around the bush. Her monster had returned, and she was certain he was close.

"Alex!" Gib called, and when they saw her exit the shed, he waved to her. "Come on, slowpoke!"

He then addressed Izzi. "Can you sense where he is?"

"No."

"Are you sure it's him? The last I heard from Leo they had no leads at all."

"It's him." She forced a smile to her face as Alex ran up to them. "Ready for that ice cream cone?"

"Double scoop?" Alex asked hopefully.

"You bet. Now go wash your hands."

"Yes, ma'am!" Alex grinned and started to dash inside, but came to an abrupt halt. "I left the radishes and tomatoes in the basket. I'll go get them."

Izzy looked at Gib and nodded before responding to Alex. "Okay, but don't dawdle."

"I won't."

Alex hurried back the way she'd come, and Gib opened the back door, speaking to Izzi as she preceded him into the house. "Are you certain? Could it be your mind playing tricks?"

"I'm certain." Izzi toed off her shoes in the laundry room and placed them on the shoe rack before continuing to the kitchen. The moment she crossed through the doorway, she jerked to a stop, and Gib ran into her, knocking her a foot into the room.

"Sorry, I didn't expect you to–" He didn't finish the sentence.

"Hello, Gib. Isabelle." Galen smiled at them from where he stood at the kitchen sink, holding a butcher's knife in one hand, with the index finger of his free hand on the tip of the blade as if testing its sharpness.

"You were foolish to show up here," Gib said and positioned himself between Galen and Izzi. "You know I can't let you leave."

Galen chuckled. "And how, exactly, do you plan on stopping me?" He pointed the knife at the kitchen table where Gib's weapon lay, dismantled.

Izzi admired Gib's reaction. He wasn't boastful or brash, just matter-of-fact in his tone and stance. "I don't need that to stop you."

"No?" Galen smiled. "Are you sure about that?"

Galen was clearly trying to goad Gib, and Izzi feared that if he pushed hard enough, Gib would lose his cool. "Stop it." She spoke loud and in the harshest tone she could muster. "Gib's right, you shouldn't be here. How do you know I didn't access a panic button on the way in?"

"Isabelle, my love, you know I would have sensed

that. You weren't even aware I was in your lovely home."

"But I am now, and since this has always been between you and me, let's keep it that way."

"You're right about that. Does he know?" Galen gestured toward Gib with the knife.

"Know what?" Gib asked.

"About Isabelle and me, of course. Our... relationship."

"You don't have a relationship with her,"

"Not as Galen Morris, BAU agent. In that you're correct. But as the man who deflowered her, taught her what passion is, and guided her through life, I am the most long-lasting and important relationship of her life."

"That's crap and you know it," Gib argued.

"Ah, I see." Galen looked at Izzi. "You never told him the truth."

"The truth about what?" Izzi could hear a hint of suspicion in his voice.

"About how he and his psychotic twin raped me the night their father killed my mother and brother.

About them taking me from my grandparents' home when I was eleven, and again when I was fourteen. About how he let that monster he called brother beat and rape me during those times and when he had me locked in that cage."

She looked directly at Galen as she spoke. "Is that the truth you want him to know? Or would you prefer that I tell him how you always showed up and used whatever you call the ability you possess, to calm me, to make me think you wanted to protect me, but only at a price and one more insidious and humiliating that the straight-out torture and rape your twin preferred.

"Do you want me to tell him all that? Or can I simply leave it at the fact that I hate you. I hate you for what you did to me, what you made me do, and for fooling me all these years, letting me – letting all of us believe you were a man of morals and honor, when in fact, you're a sociopath who deserves the same fate as your brother."

For a moment she thought he would come at them, but after a tense moment, he smiled and looked at Gib. "What she can't bring herself to admit is that she's miffed I didn't reveal myself to her sooner. She has and always will love me. Want me. I'm the one – the only one who can take the pain away or make her feel things she's ashamed to admit she crave."

"You're right." Izzi took a step closer. "I am ashamed. Ashamed I wasn't stronger. As a child and as a teenager. I should have fought harder, forced you to kill me. But I let fear rule and for that I will always be regretful.

"But I'm no longer a child, and I now see you clearly for the monster you are. You've betrayed everyone who ever cared about you, watched lives be snuffed out for your entertainment and lust. You're not worthy of love or even pity. You're worthless."

"Me thinks she doeth protest too much," he quipped.

"Oh?" she challenged him and took one more step toward him. She was close enough now to touch him. "Then let Gib and Alex leave and then it'll just be you and me."

"Hmm, as tempting an offer as that is, I don't think so. I do want him to leave. Just not alive. And Alex is part of our family now, so she stays with us."

"She's just a child. Let her and Gib leave, or you lose it all."

"Oh? How do you figure that?"

"Because if you don't, I'll fight you until you kill me, and by then, they will be long gone."

"I won't leave you with this monster," Gib argued

and snatched up a dishtowel from the counter. He wrapped it around one hand and took a step toward Galen.

"Oh, this is priceless," Galen taunted and shoved Izzi out of the way. "You think you can take me, old man. Then come on. You want to kill me? Now's your chance."

Gib rushed at Galen, who swiped at him with the knife. Gib managed to dodge the thrust and struck out at Galen, who attacked again, this time drawing blood from Gib's upper arm. His shirt quickly turned red, but he continued to attack and evade.

Izzi screamed at Galen, "Let him go, Galen, or I swear to God I'll kill you."

He laughed and circled around Gib, putting his back to the door leading to the dining room. That's when Izzi saw Alex, peering around the doorway. She prayed the child would stay out of sight, but Alex did just the opposite.

As Gib grabbed one of the wooden candlesticks from the table, Alex suddenly leaped out. In her hand was the hatchet they used to split kindling. Before Izzi could do more than open her mouth, Alex struck and the blade sunk into the center of his back.

Galen's mouth opened in a silent howl, and his body

bowed as the hatchet bit into him. He tried to turn, and when he did, the blade pulled free. Alex swung again, this time catching him in the left thigh. Blood spurted and Gib dove at Galen.

They went down in a heap, and Galen lost his grip on the knife. It skittered across the floor as he and Gib rolled over each other, vying for dominance. Despite his injuries, Galen was strong and managed to end up on top of Gib with his hands around Gib's throat.

Izzi lunged for the knife, and Galen released Gib to dive toward her. She fell back with the knife gripped in both hands, and before he could land, Alex attacked again with the hatchet, burying it in his back.

Galen roared and whirled around. He grabbed Alex by the throat. By then, Gib was on his feet. He took hold of the handle of the hatchet and wrenched it free. He slammed it into Galen's back again, and Galen screamed and released Alex, who fell to the floor, retching and gasping for air.

"Get Alex and get out of here!" Izzi screamed a moment before Galen collapsed on top of her, impaling himself onto the knife Izzi held. It lodged in his diaphragm. He had time to gasp in shock, blink, and then collapse as the blade punctured his heart.

Izzi screamed and shoved at him as he collapsed onto her. By then, Gib had moved Alex out of the way and had hold of Galen by one arm. He dragged Galen off Izzi, and she bolted up.

"Alex, get the bandages from the bathroom. Hurry." She then jumped up and grabbed Gib's phone from the sideboard. "Call 911 while I bandage you."

He didn't argue.

Alex raced in with the bandages and first aid and Izzi got to work. None of the cuts were life-threatening, but he'd lost a lot of blood. When she finished, she looked at Alex. "Are you okay, sweetheart?"

There was a stricken look on the child's face and her entire body trembled. "Alex, sweetie, look at me," Izzi said softly. "Please."

When Alex did finally look at Izzi, tears streamed down her face. "Will God hate me for what I did?"

"Of course not, sweetheart. You were just trying to help save us."

Alex swiped her runny nose with her arm and after a couple of tries was able to form words between sobs. "But– but I helped kill someone. Just like him. He said I'd be like him because now he was my dad and he became like his dad. He said I would become like him and his brother. The one without a name."

"What else did he say?" Gib asked.

Alex wailed and covered her face with her hands.
"I'm sorry, honey." Gib reached out to touch her
gently on the leg. "You don't have to tell us, but it
might help stop anyone else from getting hurt."

Alex lowered her hands and cleared her throat. "He
said... he said that thanks to Izzi not agreeing to be
his special girl, he had to make others. One every
year on her birthday. He said if he died, they would
find who killed him and make them pay."

"What do you mean, he made others?"

"Like himself."

It suddenly appeared in her mind, so sudden and so
clear, she had to brace herself with her hands on the
floor to keep from falling. It was like getting off a
spinning ride at the fair. Everything was titled and
swirling as the memories bombarded her with their
awful truth.

"Iz, honey are you okay?"

Gib's concern gave her the strength she needed to
hang on and not be overwhelmed by the memories..
"I remember it now," Izzi said quietly, trying to keep
the emotion from her voice. "All of it. The time they

took me when I was eleven and when I was almost fifteen and the time he held me prisoner when you saved me. They took other girls and turned them into creatures under their control. They touched those children with their evil and turned them into killers.

"You mean there are girls out there killing because Galen and his twin taught them to murder?"

"They taught them to torture and kill. Yes."

"Dear God, Iz. Is that what he was going to do to you? To Alex?"

"Yes." She nodded and then pulled Alex close to her side. "But we're not of the dark, and he couldn't turn our spirits away from the light. Right, Alex?"

Izzi realized Alex was staring at Galen and didn't seem at all affected by the blood or the sight of the knife buried in his diaphragm. "Alex?"

"If he's dead, then why do I still hear him in my head?"

Izzi's gaze shot to Gib. His expression was as shocked as she felt. "Can you hear him, Alex?" he asked. "Right now?"

"Yes."

"And what's he saying."

369

"That some things are stronger than life. Some things can never die. Like what was inside of him. It's still alive."

"Where?" Izzi asked. "Where is it alive?"

"I don't know. Out there. Somewhere. He said it's always been here, and it will find a home. And when it does, it will find us. What does that mean?"

Izzi looked at Gib, and he took her hand, clasping it tightly. She smiled at him before she answered, "It means our jobs aren't done. We thought we were finished fighting the monsters, but we might not be done just yet."

"Can I fight the monsters with you?"

"When you're older, if that's what you want."

"I just want to be a regular girl with a mom and dad and a dog."

Gib gave Izzi's hand a squeeze, and when she looked at him, he smiled. "I think we might be able to manage that, don't you think?"

"Which part?"

"All of it. After we're married, I can adopt Alex, as well. She'll be our daughter."

"We're going to marry?"

"If you want."

"I do. I very much do." Izzi's voice was joyous and looked at Alex. "How about you?"

"I do, too. Just one thing."

"What?"

"Do I get to have a dog?"

Gib and Izzi both grinned at the child who'd won their hearts. "Any kind you want, kiddo," Gib promised. "If it's okay with your mom."

"Is it?" Alex looked at Izzi.

"It sure is." And for the first time in her life, Izzi felt there was a chance for her to have a happy life.

She wasn't foolish enough to believe that evil would not rear its head again. She was finally free of those monsters., but now knew there were more who needed to be found and eliminated.

He made others.

Other girls whose innocence had been stolen. Others touched by evil. Others, who, Izzi was willing to bet, would come looking for who destroyed their creators.

Izzi wasn't going to ignore the warning. She was going to be watchful, pay attention, and prepare.

For whatever came next.

A Closing Word

I've been a reader my entire life, finding solace, excitement, happiness, fear and love in the pages of books. If anything has been a constant in my life, it's reading.

I also remember all the times in my life when being able to buy a book was a luxury, a treat that I didn't get every week. I've never forgotten those times or how much those books meant to me.

That's why I am so grateful to you, the readers. Regardless of your level of income or profession, I understand how precious your reading dollars are and I feel humbled that you've used some of those dollars to purchase my books.

I hope my stories prove worthy of your investment and thank you from the bottom of my heart.

Many blessings.

Ciana

Made in the USA
Middletown, DE
06 May 2022

65427278R00215